"Ready for champagne?"

Justin asked.

"Oh, yes." Ginger met his gaze, and for the first time she didn't even try to hide her feelings. She'd never meant to play games with Justin, so tonight she owed him honesty.

Justin felt the jolt of heat and nearly spilled the sparkling wine. Maybe he wasn't so good at reading her moods after all. She definitely had the look of a woman in love. *His woman;* the only one he'd ever really wanted. He offered her a glass.

"How about a toast?" Ginger said, her excitement building as their fingers brushed on the slender stem of the glass.

"To us." Justin touched his glass to hers. He wanted to add more, but he didn't. What was happening between them was too fragile, the feelings were too new.

"To us." She echoed his words, thinking them over. Could "they" be an "us"? Would it really work out somehow? She desperately wanted to believe that they could find a way....

Dear Reader,

Welcome to Silhouette Romance—experience the magic of the wonderful world where two people fall in love. Meet heroines who will make you cheer for their happiness, and heroes (be they the boy next door or a handsome, mysterious stranger) who will win your heart. Silhouette Romance novels reflect the magic of love—sweeping you away with books that will make you laugh and cry, heartwarming, poignant stories that will move you time and time again.

In the next few months, we're publishing romances by many of your all-time favorites such as Diana Palmer, Brittany Young, Annette Broadrick and many others. Your response to these authors and other authors in Silhouette Romance has served as a touchstone for us, and we're pleased to bring you more books with Silhouette's distinctive medley of charm, wit and—above all—*romance*.

During 1991, we have many special events planned. Don't miss our WRITTEN IN THE STARS series. Each month in 1991, we're proud to present readers with a book that focuses on the hero—and his astrological sign.

I hope you'll enjoy this book and all of the stories to come. Come home to romance—Silhouette Romance—for always!

Sincerely,

Tara Gavin
Senior Editor

BLYTHE STEPHENS

Gift of Mischief

Silhouette Romance

Published by Silhouette Books New York

America's Publisher of Contemporary Romance

To Muffie,
who was my own
Little Mischief

SILHOUETTE BOOKS
300 E. 42nd St., New York, N.Y. 10017

GIFT OF MISCHIEF

ISBN: 0-373-08786-1

First Silhouette Books printing April 1991

Printed in the U.S.A.

Books by Blythe Stephens

Silhouette Special Edition
Rainbow Days #554

Silhouette Romance
Gift of Mischief #786

BLYTHE STEPHENS

penned her first story when she was in third grade. Years later, after college and marriage, she became seriously involved with writing and published several short pieces. She soon discovered that novels were more fun, and with over fifty published books, she hasn't returned to the short-story form. Her books range from children's and young adult—including a few Nancy Drews, written under the pen name Carolyn Keene—to Gothics, historicals, family sagas and contemporary romances. She loves the challenge of trying different genres.

Born in Idaho and raised in Montana, Blythe has followed the sun and currently resides in Mesa, Arizona. She shares a home with her mother (who is also her assistant editor and chief critic) and their Cairn Terriers. Blythe enjoys reading and traveling, and is constantly seeking new settings for her books. Her only regret is that she can't travel to the past to do on-the-spot research.

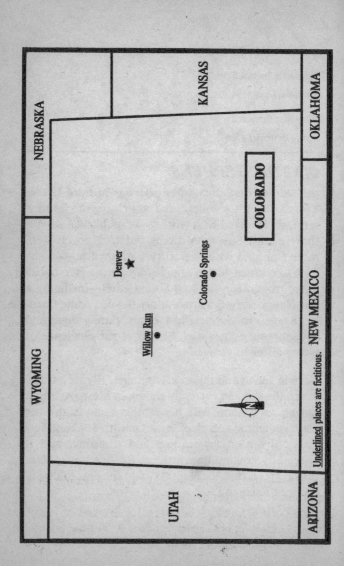

WYOMING

NEBRASKA

KANSAS

Denver ★

Willow Run ●

Colorado Springs ●

COLORADO

OKLAHOMA

UTAH

ARIZONA

NEW MEXICO

Underlined places are fictitious.

Chapter One

"I know you didn't want me to interrupt you while you're working on the contracts, Ginger, but your mother is on line one and she says she has to speak to you at once." Ann, her usually unflappable secretary, sounded concerned.

Ginger Howard frowned. Her mother called infrequently and Ginger couldn't remember the last time she'd insisted on being put right through. Usually, she was content to have Ginger call back. She pressed the proper button and tried to hide her concern with an enthusiastic greeting. "Happy New Year, Mom."

"I wish it were here, Virginia, but I'm afraid that the year is getting off to a bad start already."

Ginger swallowed a sigh. Her mother was the only person who called her Virginia; she much preferred Ginger, a nickname her father had given her as soon as he saw her ruddy curls. The old ache formed in her throat just thinking of her father, but she forced it away. Nostalgia about life with Daddy wouldn't help her deal with her mother.

"What's wrong, Mom?" she asked, a flutter of fear danc-ing in her stomach.

"It's Dena, Virginia. She called me this morning to tell me that she's in the hospital with a broken hip. She was terri-bly upset, seems she's gotten herself involved in some crazy real estate scheme and now she's going to be incapacitated for months and..." Edith Paxton's exasperated sigh re-vealed that she felt incapable of coping with what had hap-pened to the woman she'd called her best friend for as long as Ginger could remember.

"How serious is it? How did it happen? Why didn't she call me?" Ginger raked her fingers through the sophisti-cated waves she'd arranged so carefully this morning, not caring that she was releasing her untidy curls from the hair spray's control. The appointments she'd set up for the day vanished from her mind as worry about her father's sister swept through her.

"I'm sure she didn't want to worry you with her prob-lems. We both know how little time you have now that your business has become so successful."

Ginger winced at her mother's words, aware that she meant them, but plagued by guilt. Every time her mother congratulated her on her growing real estate management business, it reminded her of how she'd neglected Aunt Dena while she built up her company. Still, it was nice to know Mom admired her success even though she'd rarely ap-proved of anything else that Ginger had ever done. "So what did Dena want you to do, Mom?"

Another sigh. "She would like me to fly to Willow Run and help her out, of course, but I really can't. At least not for a while. Evan just opened the new wing of the resort and I can't leave him with everything to do. This is our busy season, you know. But still, I do worry about Dena."

Ginger closed her eyes as she listened to the details of Dena's accident. Though Ginger had only visited the Florida resort a half-dozen times in the ten years since her mother and Evan Paxton, her second husband, had bought the place, she could picture her mother perfectly. Edith Paxton, who looked a good fifteen years younger than her fifty-seven, would be gazing out at the beach with a contented smile that announced to the world that Tango Cay Resort was her dearest love.

"I'll call Aunt Dena right away," Ginger promised when her mother finished.

"Do you think you could maybe arrange for someone in Willow Run to help her? I've been away from there for so long I wouldn't even know whom to contact."

"I'll take care of it, Mom, don't worry." Ginger leaned back, asking the usual questions about Evan, the weather and the tourist season, then answered her mother's questions about Howard Management. That way, the conversation lasted a little longer without delving too deeply into either of their lives.

The fact that they both felt more comfortable discussing business depressed Ginger. But then, she thought bitterly as she replaced the receiver, how could they share any more? Her mother obviously hadn't wanted children when Ginger came along and nothing that had happened during the twenty-seven years of Ginger's life had changed her mother's feelings. She'd been Daddy's special girl until his death when she was fifteen. After that, she'd been special to nobody.

"Except maybe Aunt Dena," she reminded herself, staring at the hospital phone number her mother had given her. Her aunt had been there for her when she'd needed her those last lonely years in Willow Run, so maybe now it was her turn to be there for Dena. She gazed out at the bright California sunshine as she tried to decide what she was going to say once she reached Dena.

* * *

One week later, Ginger shivered as she eased her sports car off the main highway and around the treacherous curves that led up into the mountains to Willow Run. Why the hell couldn't Dena have broken her hip in the summer? Late January was no time for a California sun lover to be visiting the Colorado Rockies. The car slithered on the icy road as though sharing her discomfort.

It had taken her this long to make all the arrangements necessary for her partner Les Cowan to take over full control of Howard Management and now she was getting cold feet in more ways than one. Surely someone in Willow Run could have moved into Dena's house and...

She slowed even further as she reached the crest of the hill above Willow Run. The town spread out below like a Christmas card scene, the forested flanks of the mountain covered with a mantle of white while the stream that had given the town its name flowed like a dark ribbon, defying the encroaching ice on its banks.

A thousand memories filled her mind and ached like a swallowed sob in her throat. Galloping nostalgia, she told herself firmly, probably coupled with exhaustion from driving on icy roads. She was certainly out of practice after living in the Los Angeles area. She eased the sleek black car around the grove of evergreens and down the hill, suddenly eager to be home.

Justin McGovern stood at the window of the small furniture factory, staring out at the bleak slopes of the mountains, where winter lay heavy. He sighed, aware that this season wasn't going to be like other years, when there'd been few orders and winter meant hard times for the employees of McGovern Fine Furnishings. His last sales trip to Denver had resulted in a number of orders, so why was he feeling depressed instead of elated?

He ignored the cynical inner voice that suggested his dark mood had more to do with his approaching thirtieth birthday than the fortunes of the family business. He'd had such different plans for his life when he left Willow Run to go to college, plans that hadn't included coming back here to build furniture.

The dark car caught his eye as it slowed at the top of the hill. Some misguided tourist, or an optimistic skier figuring to get to the slopes this way? Envy surged through him as he watched the sleek car take the curves.

"Justin, there's a Mr. Hughes on the phone. I can't find any record of his order. Can you tell him when it will be ready?" Holly's voice dragged him away from his daydream of racing along some distant highway in the black sports car.

"I'll take it." He reached for the phone. There was no use dreaming of freedom when Holly couldn't even answer a simple customer question without him. He located the order and assured Mr. Hughes that his Victorian sofa and chairs would be ready in time for his Valentine's Day wedding anniversary.

"Justin." His sister, Holly, stood in the office doorway, her wary expression telling him even before she spoke that she was going to ask a favor.

"What now, kid?" he asked, thinking that she looked closer to sixteen than twenty. And acted it, too, when it came to taking responsibility. Sometimes he wondered if she'd ever be ready to take over and run the business.

"Do you think you could close up tonight? I know it's my turn, but Phil has these tickets for the Dark Side concert in Crestline and with the roads the way they are, we need to leave pretty early."

"You'll owe me two nights in a row next week." He couldn't turn her down, not when she looked at him with their mother's pleading blue eyes. Besides, he didn't want

Phil to be in a hurry on the road between here and Crest-line. He groaned as she disappeared through the door of the outer office—even in his thoughts, he sounded more like a father than an older brother. His broad shoulders slumped a little as he turned back to his work. Thanks to Holly and Michael, he felt more like a staid middle-aged father than a man looking forward to living a life of his own.

The restless feeling faded as he plunged into the stack of papers. There was nothing to be done about his situation, anyway; he'd accepted that five years ago when Mom died. Someone had to run the factory and take care of Holly and Michael, who'd only been thirteen then. So he'd come home to Willow Run, and here he'd stayed for five long years— and there was no end in sight, at least as far as he could see.

Later, Justin looked at his watch and cursed. Ten to one Holly had forgotten her promise to go by the Palmer place to take care of Mischief, which meant he'd better stop on his way home. He shuffled the papers around one last time, then got to his feet, not minding the errand that much. At least Mischief would be glad to see him. A man had to take his female admirers wherever he found them.

Ginger drove slowly through the familiar streets. Her visit to the hospital had eased some of her worry. Dena's bright green eyes were still full of sparkle and fight even though it was obvious that she was in pain from her hip and the mul-titude of bruises she'd gotten from her fall. It was reassur-ing to know it took more than a broken hip and nearly sixty years of living to defeat her irrepressible aunt.

"Lordy, I hope I'm that tough," she murmured, sighing as she turned into the unshoveled driveway, hoping that the car would make it through the drifts to some place close to the rear door. Naturally, as a good California girl, she'd overlooked the fact that she'd need snow boots.

"Ah, damn!" Ginger fought the wheel as the car slithered, then stalled in the snow. Gritting her teeth, she tried working with the car, but either the snow was deeper than she'd thought, or she'd really lost her touch. The car wallowed and the motor roared as the tires spun, but she didn't make any progress—forward or backward.

Once she shut off the motor, the silence was deafening. Ginger leaned back and closed her eyes. Why hadn't she parked at the curb even if it was a longer walk to the front door with all her belongings? At least the sidewalk outside the fence was shoveled. The distance between where she'd stopped in the driveway and the back porch was... She peered out her window and shivered.

Three jumps, maybe four, she told herself, gathering her purse and overnight case for the first trip. So she'd get her feet wet.... Aunt Dena was bound to have some snow boots she could wear and once she shoveled a path to the car, unloading would be a piece of cake. She took a deep breath and forced the door open, skimming a layer of snow off the drift.

The icy air nearly paralyzed her lungs, which stopped the squeal of shock as her sneakered feet and nylon-covered legs disappeared into the snow. Her jumps were less than graceful and the distance proved greater than she'd thought, but she made it to the back porch without falling. Shivering and muttering curses at the fates and her mother for leaving this up to her, Ginger dug Dena's keys out of her pocket and shakily tried to find the one that fit the back door.

Just as she turned the knob, a flurry of barking erupted inside. Ginger stepped back as the door exploded outward and a stocky gray shape barreled past her down the steps and into the snow. "Mischief!"

The schnauzer didn't even look around as, belatedly, Ginger remembered Dena's parting words. "Better go in the front door, Ginger, and make sure the gate is closed. Mischief's probably pretty lonely by now.''

Cursing herself and the dog equally, Ginger dropped her purse and case inside and plunged off the porch into the snow in the wake of the floundering but obviously determined dog. Shouting Mischief's name didn't seem to even slow the beast as she headed down the driveway toward the street. Suddenly Ginger's foot hit a patch of hidden ice and went out from under her. She lurched about wildly for a moment, then tumbled into a deep drift, landing flat on her back.

Icy crystals spilled down her neck and filtered up her sleeves as a blanket of snow settled over her. Tears of frustration burned in her eyes as she struggled to lift her head. She blinked away the snow so she could see which way the blasted dog had headed. If anything should happen to Mischief... She could imagine how devastated Dena would be. Every letter and phone call for the past year had been full of references to her "darling little Mischief."

As she struggled in the snow something resembling a furry, fifteen-pound cannonball landed on her chest and a warm pink tongue swiped away the snow that had crusted on her cheek. Bright brown eyes peered at her from beneath frosty gray eyebrows. Mischief's delighted "woof" and madly wagging knob of a tail made it clear she adored this new game.

Aware that this was her chance, Ginger wrapped her arms around the dog before she could escape again. "When we're inside, I'm going to get you for this, Mischief," she confided as she tried to turn over enough to get to her knees without releasing her hold on the struggling dog.

The snow shifted and settled around her like quicksand and the wiggling dog kept her off balance. Ginger moved one hand, seeking a collar, hoping she could get Mischief off her chest and still not let her escape. Mischief gave her another swipe with her tongue, then looked around. To Ginger's horror, she began to yelp like a demented creature.

"Blast it, dog, if you keep jumping up and down on me, I'll never get up and so help me, I'll hold on to you so we freeze together, you..."

"What the heck are you doing to Mischief?" The man was shouting; otherwise, she'd never have heard him over the racket.

Ginger gasped as the dog was suddenly jerked from her grasp. Mischief seemed delighted to be tucked under the man's arm—at least she stopped her yelping. Dazed, Ginger looked up at the stranger.

His face was too shadowed for her to see clearly, but he looked ominously tall silhouetted against the cloudy gray sky. Still, when he leaned down to offer her his free hand, she grasped it eagerly. Mischief barked with excitement as Ginger nearly pulled her would-be rescuer into the snow with her while she struggled to get her feet under her.

"Mischief, behave yourself," the man ordered firmly and to Ginger's surprise the dog immediately subsided into silence.

Ginger took a deep breath, shivering as more snow filtered down her neck when she shook her head. She rubbed her eyes, trying to clear away the snow still caught in her eyelashes. "I want to thank you for... Justin!"

"Ginger?" His frown brought his thick black brows together over his thundercloud gray eyes. "Is that really you under all that snow?"

Suddenly the pure absurdity of the situation washed over her, bringing with it a tide of laughter. "Who else would be crazy enough to be ambushed by that maniacal mutt?" Her giggles sounded slightly hysterical, but she couldn't help that. Of all the people she'd known long ago in Willow Run, Justin McGovern was positively the last one she'd expected to see today.

"Mischief's just feeling housebound," Justin explained. "Let me put her in the yard." He carried the wiggling dog to the fence that enclosed the front yard, leaning over it to drop Mischief into the soft snow. The dog raced away through the drifts like a small bulldozer, pausing only for an occasional bark.

Ginger studied Justin as he turned back to face her. He looked different. Older, of course, and more attractive now that he'd grown into the craggy features that had seemed too blunt on a teenage boy. But it was more than just the changes time made. He looked . . .

"Did you freeze to the spot, Howard, or do you enjoy making snow angels in your city clothes?" His tone seemed surprisingly familiar. "You'd better get inside and start drying off before you turn into a sexy icicle."

Justin kept his tone light as he held out his hand to her again, but he couldn't ignore the flare of warmth that spread through him the moment he touched her icy fingers. It came as a shock to discover that the grown-up Ginger Howard was even more appealing than the teenager he'd known when they were both still in high school.

"If you find icicles sexy, you've been here too long, McGovern." Ginger tried to match his casual tone even as electric currents warmed her frozen skin. This was good old Justin rescuing her, not some mysterious or exciting stranger. So why did her pulse rate accelerate when he slipped a strong arm around her waist to keep her on her feet as they headed for the back door, which she'd left standing open?

"What in the world do you have on your feet?" Justin caught a glimpse of her shoes as they reached the furrows plowed by the car. He could feel her shivers as he pressed her tight against his side to keep her from falling again.

Ginger sighed. "Sneakers."

"California girls." Justin shook his head, resisting an urge to simply pick her up and carry her to the back porch. The Ginger he remembered had been far too independent to allow anyone to help her and he already sensed the tension his practical embrace was producing. She'd pull away and end up in another snowdrift if he didn't divert her attention. "Did you forget what winter is like in Colorado?"

"I got rid of all my heavy clothes because I never intended to spend another winter in Colorado." She tried to keep her tone light, but she was having difficulty concentrating. Probably the result of the cold. At least, she didn't want to think it had anything to do with being pressed against Justin's warm side. It annoyed her to realize that she was actually enjoying his protectiveness. "What are you doing here? Not that I don't appreciate the rescue."

"I just came by to check on Mischief. I've been trying to spend a little time with her since Dena's been in the hospital. Even though she has a doggy door to the backyard, she gets pretty lonesome and bored here alone and with Mischief, that can be a lethal combination."

Ginger looked up at him, noticing the laugh wrinkles at the corner of his eye. And his grin softened the hard line of his mouth in a way that definitely was different than she remembered. Not that she actually remembered much about Justin McGovern. In high school he'd been far too serious to interest her.

Suddenly aware that they'd reached the porch and Justin was still holding her close, Ginger eased away from his side. "I thought Dena told me Sandy was taking care of the dog."

"She comes over to see her a couple of times during the day, but with the snow so deep, it's pretty hard for her to get around and Mischief and I are buddies." Justin relinquished his hold on her as she stepped inside and switched on the kitchen light. Sensing a change in Ginger's mood, he made no move to follow her.

"Aren't you coming in?" Ginger stopped halfway across the spotless tile, suddenly aware that she was leaving a definite trail as the snow melted off her sneakers and dropped in chunks from her crusted tweed suit.

"I was thinking that I might unload your car first." Justin had already recognized the sports car as the one he'd been watching earlier. "I might even dig it out of that drift for you."

"I was on my way in to get a pair of Dena's boots so I could do that, when the dog got loose and..." Ginger trailed off, embarrassed by her sudden need to explain her actions. Since when did it matter to her what anyone else thought? The draft from the open door made her shiver.

Justin grinned at her. This was definitely the Ginger he remembered, as thornily independent as ever. "In the interest of keeping you from getting pneumonia, why don't you just let me unload the car while you take a hot shower and change into something dry? You can shovel the car out if you really want to do it, but I don't think Dena will appreciate having you sick when she gets out of the hospital."

For a moment she felt a familiar surge of anger at his teasing words, then the ridiculousness of her protests overrode her habitual need to depend on no one but herself. She caught the sparkle of laughter in his eyes and responded with a smile of gratitude. "Well, just this once, as a favor to Aunt Dena, I guess I could let you dig the car out for me, especially if you'll park it on the street. I'd probably just get it stuck again before I got out of the driveway. I've really lost my touch for driving in snow and ice."

"So go dry off before the chill gets any worse." Justin forced himself to close the door between them. How the devil did she manage to look so appealing when she was dripping wet and shivering so hard she could scarcely stand? And where was his protectiveness coming from? Ginger was just here to take care of her aunt. Once Dena was well, she'd be heading back to her exciting life in sunny California.

Envy tugged at him as he moved to the open sports car. If he'd been able to stay with the computer firm in Denver, he'd probably be driving a sports car, too. He'd been in line for a management position when Mom's heart attack... He forced the thoughts away. Might-have-beens didn't change anything and Ginger would need her own clothes to change into. Nothing of Dena's would fit the trim figure he'd seen outlined by the soggy wool suit.

Memories of the feel of her body against his side brought a stirring of heat within him. She'd definitely matured into a beautiful woman—it was surprising that she hadn't married. Unless, of course, she'd made up her mind never to marry. The Ginger he'd known in high school had never been one to settle down to steady dating.

He shook his head. The guys had called her cold and a lot of less flattering things, but he'd always had a hunch that there was a fire burning behind her facade of independence. It would be a waste if no man ever brought it to the surface. He sighed, wondering if perhaps someone already had. If some jerk had hurt her... It was none of his business.

Ginger, inside the house, shivering, slipped her feet out of her soaking wet sneakers, then shrugged off the heavy wool jacket. Her suit would never be the same, that was for sure. Carrying her dripping shoes, she hurried down the hall to her aunt's bedroom and bath. There was no point in trailing water all the way upstairs to the room that had once been hers.

Though she'd meant to hurry, it was nearly an hour later when Ginger emerged from the bedroom, comfortably wrapped in the heavy green plaid robe she'd found hanging in the closet. A hot bubble bath had eased the frost from her bones and some of the weariness from her muscles, but now she was hungry. She just hoped Aunt Dena had left a pantry full of food, since there was no way she was venturing out to buy groceries tonight—even supposing there was a store open evenings in Willow Run.

"It's about time you showed up. I was beginning to think I was going to have to send Mischief in to see if you'd drowned."

Ginger jumped and whirled around, then looked up to discover Justin standing on the stairs, looking very much at home. Irritation swept through her, especially when she realized just how she must look in the ratty old robe with her damp hair curling wildly around her face. She'd assumed that he'd have left long ago, having done his good deeds for the day.

"Sorry, I didn't mean to startle you." Justin grinned at her. "I just took your suitcases up to your room. You ready for hot chocolate and cinnamon toast?"

"What?" She noticed he'd shed his heavy jacket. He looked good without it, his wide shoulders emphasized by the Nordic design of his red, black and white ski sweater. His weathered jeans were damp to the knees and he'd taken off his boots to pad around in bright-patterned red-and-white socks.

"Aren't you hungry? I guess I should have asked, but I remembered that you had a fondness for hot chocolate and my cinnamon toast." Justin studied her, fascinated by the momentary play of emotions he could read on her face. Her wide hazel eyes seemed soft and vulnerable when she was startled, but that changed too quickly. Her polite smile remained, but her guard was back in place and he could read nothing of what she was feeling. Not that she wasn't still appealing, with her cheeks ruddy from the heat of her bath and her skin glowing in a way that made him want to stroke...

"Cinnamon toast." Ginger swallowed hard as memories ambushed her.

Without warning, she slipped back in time, to relive the night of the junior prom. She'd been on cloud nine when Jeff Hudson, one of the most popular senior boys, had asked her to be his date. It was only later, when he'd insisted that they leave the dance early to park up on the hill, that she'd realized there was more to his invitation than a desire for her company.

Justin watched her face become still and closed and cursed himself for a fool. Why the heck hadn't he kept his mouth shut? How could he have forgotten what had led up to their midnight chocolate-and-toast party in his mother's kitchen? Or had he wanted to forget that he'd found her walking home from Makeout Hill that long-ago night, her dress mussed and tears streaking her makeup?

At the time he'd wanted to find Jeff Hudson and kill him for hurting Ginger with his clumsy pass, but instead he'd simply taken her to his house. Feeling hopelessly inadequate, he'd offered cocoa, toast and his shoulder to cry on. Luckily, it had been enough. Before he took her home, she'd been able to laugh as she told him about taking Jeff's car keys and throwing them down the hill before she started to walk home. Being with her, listening to her confidences and making her feel better about herself had made that night a special memory for him, but it had undoubtedly affected her differently.

"Are you telling me you're not hungry?" he asked, suddenly aware that the silence was stretching too long between them. "Or don't you trust me in the kitchen?"

"I'm starving." Ginger forced the sour memories away, hoping Justin didn't remember how vulnerable she'd been that long-ago night. Past was past; she wasn't so easily fooled these days. The current Ginger Howard never let anyone get close enough to hurt her the way Jeff Hudson had. She gave Justin a reassuring smile. "Let me get into some dry clothes and I'll be delighted to eat everything in sight. Wallowing in all that snow really gave me an appetite."

Justin felt a mixture of regret and relief as Ginger brushed by him, then ran up the stairs leaving a dizzying scent of lilacs around him. Had he been wrong about her remembering that night? Maybe it hadn't meant anything special to her. As he headed for the kitchen he wondered why he'd never been able to forget it.

Chapter Two

Unpacking and donning wool slacks and a bulky gold pullover didn't take long, but Ginger gave extra care to her hair and makeup, suddenly needing the reassurance of her normally perfect grooming. It wasn't that she wanted to impress Justin, she assured herself; she just couldn't bear to have him think she always looked like something he'd pulled out of a snowdrift.

As she subdued her willful curls, she found herself wondering about Justin. Dena had mentioned his name in her letters from time to time, but Ginger hadn't paid much attention to the facts of his life. She'd long ago relegated him to the past she'd planned to forget once she left Willow Run.

Not that Justin had been in Willow Run at the time she'd set out to conquer the world. As a matter of fact, she couldn't remember seeing him again during the two years following his graduation from good old Willow Run High. So what was he doing here now? Why had he come back? Had he returned to marry a local girl or . . .

She frowned at her reflection, then threw down the brush. This was silly. If she wanted to know, all she had to do was go downstairs and ask him. Besides, she'd come home to take care of Aunt Dena, nothing else.

A flurry of barking erupted just as she opened her bedroom door, and she heard the low rumble of Justin's voice as he commanded Mischief to be quiet. The barking subsided into a series of yelps and whines as the front door opened and closed.

"Is that Ginger's car out front, Justin? I just called Dena and she said that Ginger finally got into town."

"Sandy!" Her speculation about Justin disappeared in a quick wash of pleasure as Ginger recognized her one-time best friend's voice. "Sandy, is that really you?" Visions of the blond, blue-eyed girl from up the street filled her mind as she raced down the stairs and into the living room, then skidded to a halt, gasping in shock.

"Yes, Ginger, it's really me." Sandy's eyes sparkled with laughter as she held out her arms. "Welcome home, stranger."

Giggling, Ginger gave her friend a careful hug. "I didn't realize.... Justin said something about it being hard for you to get around in the snow, but..."

"But nothing to prepare you for the fact that skinny old Sandy is now doing a whale imitation," Sandy finished for her, patting her extremely pregnant stomach. "I keep telling Dr. Ellis that it must be twins, but he says no."

Justin chuckled. "As I recall, that's what he told Betty Carter a couple of years ago. I'm not sure the old guy can count."

Sandy waddled to a chair and sank down with a sigh. "I wish people would quit telling me that. I wanted twins before Joey was born, but I don't need two babies with a three-year-old in the house."

"Joey is three already?" Ginger settled herself on the couch, her first glow of happiness fading a little as the years they'd been apart intruded on her memories of closeness with Sandy. She'd come home for Sandy and Robert's wedding six years ago, but since then their only contact had been occasional letters and phone calls. Her weariness returned.

"Don't look so shocked. I have trouble believing it, too." Sandy's pixie grin hadn't changed; the warmth was still there. "So how are you? How long can you stay? What do you think of the old town?"

"While you're answering Sandy's questions, why don't I get the food?" Justin's question snapped Ginger's attention back to him.

"Oh, I'll help you." Ginger got up, heat rising in her cheeks. She, not Justin, should be taking charge, offering refreshments to her guests. It embarrassed her to realize that Justin seemed far more at home in her aunt's house than she was.

"No need. Everything is about ready." Justin headed for the kitchen, telling himself that he should be grateful for Sandy's arrival. She'd bring Ginger up to date on all their old friends and give him a chance to slip away without feeling that he was deserting her. After all, he had brought some invoices to go over and he'd promised his brother, Michael, that they'd watch the basketball game together later.

Somehow neither prospect sounded the slightest bit interesting now, though he wasn't sure why. There was certainly no reason for him to stick around listening to Sandy and Ginger gossip and giggle like Holly and her girlfriends. He'd just stopped by to feed the dog and play with her for a while—entertaining Ginger hadn't been a part of his plans.

Not that she'd want him to stick around anyway, he reminded himself. She never had when they were teenagers, and it seemed unlikely that age had softened her self-protective shell. Still, coming all the way from California to stay in an empty house couldn't be much fun and Sandy probably wouldn't be able to stay long. Besides, he was hungry and he'd found a cache of Dena's molasses cookies in the cupboard. No man could be expected to resist that kind of temptation.

Ginger dropped back on the couch and tried to concentrate on Sandy's words, but her thoughts kept straying after Justin. She shouldn't be just sitting here like a guest while he played host. It was bad enough that he'd had to rescue her from the snowdrift and dig her car out after she got it stuck; there was absolutely no reason he should . . .

"So why don't you just go out and help him?" Sandy's soft whisper brought her back to the conversation she was supposed to be having with her friend.

"What?" Ginger tried for a look of innocent confusion.

"Come on, you haven't heard a word I've said. Go, I'll still be here. Lord knows, I'm in no hurry to move." Sandy's grin brought back a thousand memories of shared secrets and teenage plotting.

"I really should be helping him," Ginger conceded, suddenly not caring that Sandy had noticed her preoccupation. "He's been so nice to me since I got here."

"Besides that he's really grown up into a handsome devil." Sandy's mischievous grin accompanied her whisper. "Even we old married women have noticed that, Ginger."

Ginger tried to come up with a quip that would make her lack of interest in Justin perfectly clear, but her brain seemed to have decided to take a vacation. She'd have to clue Sandy in later. No way could she ever become romantically interested in Justin McGovern or anyone else in Willow Run.

He sensed her presence the moment she entered the kitchen. "Too hungry to wait?" he teased.

"Too guilty. You should be in there resting up after all that snow shoveling. I really do appreciate what you did for me, Justin. I'd have been half the day tomorrow getting the car out. And, of course, you rescued me from Mischief. Aunt Dena never told me that she was attack trained." She stopped, suddenly aware that she was chattering like a nervous teenager. When she looked into those warm gray eyes, her tongue seemed to slip into overdrive. How come she hadn't remembered that Justin had such devastatingly long eyelashes?

"The pleasure was all mine." His deepening grin further softened the hard planes of his face, quickening her pulse rate. "It isn't every day I find an old friend buried in the snow."

Ginger was sorry when he turned his attention back to the tray of food. What the heck was the matter with her? Did she actually want Justin to be attracted to her? Was she that desperate for attention now that she was back in Willow Run?

That thought brought a chill that had nothing to do with the outside temperature. Just being here couldn't have sent her emotionally back in time, could it? She shivered. No way would she ever again allow herself to be the insecure and lonely teenager who'd fled the confining atmosphere of Willow Run.

The tray ready, Justin allowed himself to watch her. He was intrigued by the way tendrils of auburn hair curled around her face and by the fan of her dark lashes against her golden cheeks as she looked down, hiding her eyes from his gaze. He sensed that something was bothering her, but he hadn't a clue to what it might be.

He hurried to fill the silence that stretched between them. "By the way, Ginger, I'll come over sometime tomorrow and see about digging out the driveway. Your car is going to be a problem without chains or snow tires, so maybe you should use Dena's for a while. I put it in the garage for her after she fell, so..." He let it trail off, suddenly aware that she was frowning at him.

"I couldn't ask you to do that, Justin. Besides, I don't mind being in the snow when I'm dressed for it." Ginger met his gaze firmly. She'd had more than enough of feeling like a helpless female today. It was time to let Justin know that she didn't expect to be rescued anymore.

"You didn't ask me, but I certainly wouldn't want to deprive you of the pleasure of shoveling snow. I get plenty of it." He couldn't help grinning at her, remembering the innumerable times he'd heard her announce to everyone at school that she preferred to do something herself. Maybe the Ginger he remembered was still there beneath the sophisticated veneer of California career woman.

His easy acceptance of her refusal intrigued her. Most of the men she dealt with would have bristled at her tone or withdrawn with a snort of injured macho pride. Justin simply seemed amused. Was it because of their long-ago friendship or because he just didn't care enough to be disturbed by her rejecting his offer?

"Are you two going to stay out there all night?" Sandy's plaintive wail interrupted her attempt at analysis. "Mischief and I are getting lonesome."

"Food's on the way," Justin called, picking up the tray. "Unless there's something else?" He met Ginger's gaze, sensing that he'd managed to disturb her a little. The thought pleased him for some strange reason.

The sharing of the food and Sandy's lighthearted gossip quickly eased the odd tension that Ginger had sensed just before she and Justin left the kitchen. In fact, the rich flow of memories soon had her giggling like the teenager she'd been the last time they were all together. Perhaps there had been more good times than she'd remembered, she decided with a wry grin. Maybe the dark days had just overshadowed them in her memory.

She was having so much fun she resented the phone call that interrupted them and called Justin away to watch a basketball game with his brother. Not that she'd really expected him to stay this long after Sandy arrived, but the house seemed emptier after he left.

Sandy leaned back in her chair with a groan. "I should probably be going, too. You must be tired from your long trip."

"Stay awhile, please. I mean, unless you think Joey or Robert would mind." Ginger stopped, stunned by her own words. Since when did she beg for company? She'd lived alone from the moment she'd been able to manage the rent by herself, and she rarely felt lonely.

"Joey had better be asleep by now and Robert will be staring at that basketball game, too." Sandy's blue eyes narrowed. "What do you think of the grown-up version of Justin, anyway? Did you ever in your wildest dreams believe he'd turn out to be such a hunk?"

"I sure didn't expect him to end up in Willow Run." The words were out before she thought and she could see at once that they'd hurt Sandy, the last thing she'd meant to do. "I mean, he left right after high school. I thought he'd probably make a life for himself in Denver after he graduated from Denver University."

"Dena didn't tell you the story?" Sandy's gaze turned speculative, making Ginger wish she'd kept her curiosity to herself. This was the time she was supposed to be making it clear that she had no interest in Justin McGovern.

"She probably did, but I don't remember." That sounded properly uninterested, but when Sandy didn't go on she couldn't help adding, "What story?"

"It was really sad. Justin was doing great with some big computer firm in Denver, up for a fancy promotion or something. Anyway, his mom had a heart attack in her office at the furniture factory and died the next day.''

Ginger winced at the words, remembering how close Justin had been to his mother, probably because his father had deserted the family just after his little brother Michael's birth. Now that she thought about it, that was probably the reason Justin had been so serious in high school—a fact that had escaped her at the time. She forced her mind back to the present. "That must have been awful for them. When did it happen?"

"About five years ago. Holly was fifteen and Michael was just thirteen. Anyway, Justin came back and took over. He had a rough time getting the factory back on its feet. Robert said the place was really in bad shape when Mrs. McGovern died—not even salable. Now, of course, he could probably make a good profit if he decided to sell, but I expect he's hoping either Michael or Holly will want to come in with him. After all, it is a family enterprise."

Ginger nodded, compassion spilling through her as she pictured herself in Justin's position. What if Aunt Dena had needed her when Howard Management was just getting started? Would she have come home and settled down in Willow Run to take care of her? Not likely. But then, she soothed her conscience, Aunt Dena wasn't a teenager and she didn't have any family business that had to be run. Or she hadn't until recently, she reminded herself, thinking about the other problem she was going to have to deal with.

"So aren't you going to ask me about his personal life?" Sandy broke into her thoughts, reminding her that she had better set her friend straight before she made some wrong assumptions and decided to play matchmaker.

"Why?" Ginger produced her best bland smile.

Sandy frowned. "You aren't even a tiny bit curious?"

"I'm here to help Dena, Sandy, nothing more. I left a thriving business in the hands of my new partner, but I have to get back and keep an eye on things. Les is good, but he doesn't have much experience recruiting new management properties.''

Sandy responded exactly as she'd hoped. "Who is Les?"

"Les Cowan. We met at a real estate seminar in L.A. He'd been mostly in sales and had done pretty well, but was looking for something else. I started out by managing a couple of office buildings he'd been trying to sell and ended up letting him buy into the business so I could expand it.'' That was a short version of what had actually been a fairly long association that had only recently graduated from casual friendship to business.

"Partners in more than just management?" Sandy's curiosity knew no bounds, but Ginger didn't resent it.

"Les went through a nasty divorce a year ago, so we're still at the 'just friends' stage." *And we're likely to stay that way forever,* Ginger added to herself, feeling mildly guilty for letting Sandy think otherwise. Les was a terrific friend, but she knew from the months of their acquaintance that he could never be anything more. As a career woman, she had no time or desire for romance.

"Well, I'm going to tell you about Justin even if you're not interested, so listen up. Justin is unattached and seems determined to stay that way in spite of being hotly pursued by nearly every eligible female in town. He dates, but no one steady. It keeps the gossips happy, but frustrates the heck out of the women.'' Sandy giggled. "Some things never change."

"*A lot* of things never change." Ginger looked around the comfortable living room. "It's sort of scary coming back here, you know. I mean, sometimes I feel like I never left."

"Which reminds me, you never did tell me how long you were going to stay, Ginger." Sandy's expression became sober. "You aren't just here for a couple of days, are you?''

"I honestly don't know. A lot will depend on how well Dena can get along on her own. Dr. Ellis doesn't seem to know how she'll manage once I get her home. If she has problems, I'll probably have to hire someone to stay with her for a while after I go back." Ginger paused. "You don't happen to know of anyone I might get, do you?"

Sandy shook her head. "Angela used to do that, but then she married Chet Warren and now she's almost as pregnant as I am."

"No one is that pregnant," Ginger teased. "When are you due, anyway?"

"Wait till you're pregnant, Ginger, then you won't make jokes." Sandy yawned. "Dr. Ellis says some time in February, so I'm hoping for soon. Tomorrow would be nice."

"Gee, then I could visit you at the hospital when I go see Aunt Dena. That would be handy." Ginger hoped her grin covered the odd pain she felt at Sandy's warning. She never expected to be pregnant, since she knew nothing whatsoever about babies and had no interest in learning. Besides, she'd probably make a lousy mom, considering the role model her mother had been.

"Handier than the house across the street?"

"What?"

"To visit, silly. Last summer Robert and I bought the old Smith place across the street. You can visit me there even after you bring Dena home."

"Couldn't bear to leave the neighborhood, huh? I'd know these things if you'd written anything besides your name on your Christmas card this year."

"Christmas kind of got away from me. I figured I could write everybody a nice, long letter after the baby came."

"As I recall, I didn't hear from you for a year after I got Joey's birth announcement." The sparring felt as comfortably familiar as the house and the town.

"I've had more practice and this time—" Sandy stopped as someone knocked on the front door.

Ginger hurried to answer, grinning as she recognized Robert Wallace on her front porch. "Come in and join the party," she invited as soon as they'd exchanged greetings.

"Can't, I left Joey alone. I just thought I should come help my wife home. It's pretty slick crossing the street."

"He's a worrywart," Sandy murmured as Robert helped her to her feet, then held her coat for her. "For some reason he doesn't think I'm as graceful as I used to be."

"I can't imagine why." Ginger watched the two closely, noting the gentle way Robert cradled Sandy against his side, the tenderness in his face as he helped her down the front steps. And she could see Sandy returned his love—her glow lit the dark street. Even as they called their good-nights she felt like an outsider.

She was an outsider, she reminded herself as she closed and locked the door. She'd chosen to leave Willow Run, to make a different kind of life for herself, so why should she expect to belong here? She didn't want to be like Sandy and Justin and everyone else here—did she?

Ginger shook her head and began gathering up the dishes. The fact that she even asked that question told her how tired she was. She looked at her watch as Mischief disappeared out her doggy door to the backyard. It was still early by California standards, but in Willow Run they took up the streets before the ten o'clock news, so she might as well go to bed.

Going to bed early resulted in her rising before it was decent, a fact that pleased Mischief, anyway. After sharing Ginger's bacon and eggs, the dog settled down in the front yard to supervise while Ginger attacked the battered but still deadly drifts in the driveway. Snow seemed to have gotten heavier in the years she'd been away and she could now understand just how Justin had cultivated such impressive muscles.

By ten-thirty, Ginger had cleared the entire driveway and squeezed her car into the garage beside Dena's heavy sedan. "Coffee break time, Mischief," she called to the schnauzer. "I'll let you in the front door, okay?"

Talking to a dog? she asked herself as she limped up the back steps and cautiously pulled her frozen feet out of Dena's one-size-too-large snow boots. She'd caught herself directing comments to the mutt all morning, but did she really expect the dog to be waiting for her at the front door?

The yip came before she was halfway across the living room. Mischief obviously thought she was too slow. Ginger grinned as she opened the door and picked up the grimy towel Justin had used to dry the dog yesterday. "Had enough of the cold, too?"

The dog's bright eyes met hers as she dried the furry paws then gave her a quick, all-over rub. Whether or not the dog understood every word she said—and Dena contended she did—Mischief was an attentive listener.

"I could use a friend like you at home," Ginger confided, scratching behind the uncropped ears. "Of course, I'm really not in my apartment enough to take care of a dog, but it would be nice to have someone to talk to when I get home."

Mischief sneezed, then followed Ginger to the kitchen to see if anything had magically appeared in her dish since her morning portion of dry food. Finding nothing, she joined Ginger in the big chair in the living room. Ginger sighed, took a sip of coffee, then picked up the phone. She'd put off her call to Florida as long as she could. Unfortunately, she found it much easier to talk to Mischief than to her mother.

The conversation went pretty much as expected. She answered questions about Dena's condition and prospects for release from the hospital, then listened to several minutes of advice. Just as she was about to hang up, her mother asked, "How are you, Virginia—are you glad to be back in Willow Run?"

"Glad? Why would I be? I just came to take care of Aunt Dena." Ginger stopped petting the dog, shocked that her mother would even ask such a question.

"I thought maybe you would be glad to have a reason to visit. You've been away for a long time and I can remember when you definitely preferred Willow Run to any place else on earth." The angry note in her mother's voice surprised her.

"At that time I hadn't exactly been many other places," Ginger reminded her, wondering where this conversation might be going.

"Well, you certainly preferred it to Florida." The anger became bitterness. "You couldn't wait to get back there, back to Dena."

"I was sixteen and all my friends were here." Anger blazed inside her, but Ginger swallowed the well-remembered protests. This argument was eleven years out of date. "Why are you bringing this up now, Mom?" she asked.

"Just curious, that's all. Well, I've got to go. Evan is at the airport picking up some new arrivals and I've got to be sure their rooms are ready. Call me when you know more about Dena's condition, okay?" The phone was dead before she could reply.

Ginger shook her head as she placed the receiver back in its cradle. She'd never pretended to understand her mother, but that conversation was weird even for her. Maybe it was because she was back here—maybe Willow Run made people strange even long distance. That thought made her laugh.

"Well, I'd better go out and start a grocery list, dog." She started to shift the snuggling schnauzer off her lap, then sighed as the telephone rang. "Saved by the bell, Mischief."

"Ginger?"

She had no trouble recognizing Justin's voice.

"Unless the dog answers the phone, you'd better hope it's me," she told him. "What's up?"

"I was wondering if you'd like to go out for dinner tonight? I mean, Dena's not going to be home for a couple of days and there is actually a pretty fair Western dance band at the Candlelight on weekends, so..." He seemed to run out of words suddenly.

A half-dozen valid excuses sprang to mind as she considered all the reasons she had to refuse his invitation. Then she heard herself say, "I'd love to, Justin. What time?"

Justin leaned back in his chair and put his feet up on the desk. He'd done it! He'd actually invited Ginger out to dinner and she'd accepted. Things were definitely looking up.

"Justin, I was wondering..." Cynthia, the company secretary, paused in the office doorway, no doubt stunned by his idiotic grin and relaxed posture.

Justin sobered, immediately planting his shoes firmly on the stained carpet under his desk. "What is it, Cynthia?"

"Holly gave me a batch of orders and I can't figure out what this is." Cynthia's brown eyes warmed as she brought the papers to his desk. Her long blond hair brushed his shoulder as she leaned close enough for him to catch the exotic scent that radiated from her well-curved body.

Justin controlled a sigh of exasperation. He'd offered Cynthia the job three months ago for two reasons—he'd needed a secretary, and he'd felt sorry for her after her divorce. He definitely hadn't planned to heal her loneliness, and her less-than-subtle attempts at flirting were beginning to bug him.

By the time he'd finished straightening out both Holly and Cynthia, Justin's good mood had soured. He must have had an attack of temporary insanity to call Ginger Howard for a date. He didn't need any more distractions, and she certainly wasn't interested in him—a fact he'd faced painfully back in high school.

But she'd accepted. His gloom lifted as his mind filled with images of Ginger lying in the snowdrift with Mischief bouncing up and down on her midsection. She'd looked so cute with her rosy cheeks and the snow diamonds sparkling in her fiery hair and her lips...

He started as the telephone rang. Daydreaming? He tried to laugh at himself, but the thought was too unsettling. He hadn't spent time mooning over a woman since...since he couldn't remember when.

Ginger yawned as she pulled into the slushy parking lot that served the Willow Run Hospital and Clinic. She was satiated by the conversation and lunch that Sandy had offered her, but that was no excuse for the way her mind kept wandering from her concern about Dena. Instead of concentrating on what she was going to tell her aunt, she kept thinking about tonight. What on earth had possessed her to accept a date with Justin McGovern?

And she really wanted to go. That was what blew her mind. Crazy though it might be, she was actually looking forward to spending the evening at the Candlelight Supper Club with Justin and no amount of discussing it with Sandy had changed the feeling. That meant only one thing—coming to Willow Run had unhinged her mind.

At least talking to Sandy had helped her understand why Justin had called. Sandy's theory that Justin was bored with the local women and as curious about her as she was about him sounded right. Ginger could accept the fact that he might be looking for a little romance to alleviate his midwinter blues. But figuring out why he'd invited her wasn't the problem—what she needed was a logical reason for her acceptance.

Ah, yes, that was what kept itching in her mind, distracting her from everything else. Well, not quite everything. Analyzing Justin's motives didn't explain the quivery feeling she'd experienced when he'd rescued her from the snowdrift and again when they were alone in the kitchen.

Not that it mattered, she told herself, firmly forcing such thoughts from her mind. She was here to help her aunt, not to worry about vagrant quivers of . . . whatever. She parked Dena's sedan and mustered up a smile as she went inside. Men who gave her quivery feelings had no place in her busy life.

Chapter Three

"**W**ell, don't you look better already," Dena greeted her with a smile that positively glowed. "I think being home agrees with you, Ginger."

Now that was a truly frightening thought, but Ginger did her best to hide her reservations behind a smile. "You are looking at the results of a two-hour lunch with Sandy. Her cooking has definitely improved."

"Picked up right where you left off, didn't you?" Dena beamed her approval. "She's missed you."

"I've missed her, too. I just didn't realize it." The confession slipped out as she began unloading the half-dozen items that Dena had requested. To cover her lapse, she quickly moved on to relaying the messages for Dena that her mother had given her.

It took about twenty minutes to run out of small talk. Ginger squirmed on the chair as she felt her aunt's gaze. Dena's radar was something else she'd forgotten; the woman had always known when something was troubling Ginger.

The silence seemed to thicken between them, but Ginger couldn't think of anything to say. There was no way she could tell Dena what was bothering her, without opening the door to a whole conversation she wasn't ready to have.

Knowing that she had to distract her aunt before she started asking questions, Ginger decided it was time to find out more about Dena's other problem. "So why don't you tell me about this real estate venture you're involved in."

This time it was Dena who seemed to feel uncomfortable—at least, she appeared to develop a sudden fascination with pleating her bed jacket. Ginger waited, expecting to hear either details of the extravagant plans Dena had hinted at when she first called her or confirmation of the troubling possibilities her mother had suggested during their conversations. But Dena said nothing.

"The sale is complete, isn't it? I mean, this isn't a contract that could be voided because of your accident?" Hope flared at the thought of extricating her aunt.

"I wouldn't give up the inn even if I could." Dena's usually soft features took on a stubborn cast that made her look close to sixty, instead of her usual ten years younger.

"But what in the world are you going to do with it?" It took all Ginger's self-control to keep her disapproval from showing in her voice. "It's a disaster, Dena. It never was a success, so why do you think that you of all people..."

The look of pain crossing her aunt's face stopped her midsentence, the implication of her words shaming her. Blast her runaway tongue! She tried for words that would soften her unkind evaluation. "I mean, you have no experience with renovation projects or with running a hotel. And it's bound to cost a fortune before you can even hope to open the place."

Dena straightened, pushing impatiently at escaping strands of silver-threaded sable hair. Her green eyes fairly blazed with defiance. "I had to save it, Ginger. They were going to bulldoze the inn and build some kind of condo units there. Can you imagine? I saw the plans. They were all glass and concrete without any character. The stream would have been diverted and the falls destroyed. I just couldn't let it happen."

"Fancy condo units in Willow Run? To whom did they plan to sell them?" She was too shocked to hide her skepticism.

"That's right, you wouldn't know about Snow Shadow. That's the new ski area opening up just outside of Crestline. It should be in full operation by next winter. They already have some of the facilities in place."

"That's still about forty miles round trip to ski." Ginger fought the first stirring of genuine interest in the project.

"There's more." Dena's excitement revived. "I've talked to a couple of people in town about the possibility of developing this area for cross-country skiing. And then there's Willow Lake less than a mile from the inn—I want to build a small dock there and make sure that the lake is properly stocked with fish."

"Add a few rental boats, get someone to teach waterskiing and you'd have a strong year-round business," Ginger finished for her, giving in to the admiration that completely overwhelmed her doubts. "You wily little fox. Why in the world didn't you tell Mom all this? She is absolutely convinced you're going to end up bankrupt."

"Edith tends to jump to conclusions." Dena's smug smile broadened, then slowly ebbed away, and she sighed. "Anyway, there's a possibility that she could be right. I mean, the inn development has wonderful potential, but if I'm going to be hitched to a walker for a while, I could lose my shirt, Ginger. The scope of my plans requires that I be fully mobile and able to supervise and handle every detail. I didn't take my brittle bones into consideration when I signed all those papers."

"You don't have any partners in the deal?"

"I didn't have time to find any."

Ginger's feeling of impending disaster returned as she listened to Dena's description of the deal she'd made for the old, long-closed Willow Run Inn. If it had been anybody but Dena, she would have simply shaken her head in despair and walked away.

As it was, Ginger was honestly relieved when several of Dena's bridge buddies came in to visit, giving her an opportunity to escape without voicing her doubts. Hearing Ginger's opinion of her investment would undoubtedly have set Dena's recovery back by a week at least. As it was, she promised to come back and talk further tomorrow, then headed out into the cold sunshine. She needed at least twenty-four hours to figure out how she could soften the blow.

First she needed to drive out and look at the inn. Maybe it wasn't the disaster she remembered. Of course, it could be worse after ten more years of neglect. That charming possibility convinced her to head for the grocery store instead. The inn would still be there tomorrow morning, so there was no reason to risk starvation. Besides, she had to get home to prepare for her date.

Ginger grinned as she pulled into the parking lot of the supermarket. A date to go to the Candlelight. She could clearly remember when that seemed the ultimate in a romantic evening. The weird part was, she was still excited by the prospect. And was Justin McGovern the romantic man of her girlish dreams?

She shook her head at her own foolishness. Justin was just an old friend who'd turned out to be a hunk and nice to boot. Anything else she might be feeling was just the result of being back in Willow Run. That decided, she concentrated on her list.

* * *

Justin parked in front of Dena's house at exactly six-thirty, then just leaned back for a moment, grinning, as he took in the neatly shoveled front walk and driveway. Ginger had done it herself, as expected. He just hoped she wouldn't be too tired to dance tonight, because he was looking forward to holding her in his arms. It had been a long time since he'd felt this excited about a first date.

Thanks to Mischief's barking, Ginger opened the door before he reached it and Justin caught his breath. Thinking about her all day hadn't prepared him for the sudden rush of pure pleasure that just seeing her sent tingling through him. She was wearing a green dress that hugged all the delicate curves her other clothes had only hinted at. And her hazel eyes glowed as she met his gaze. He couldn't take his eyes off her as he picked up the noisy dog.

"It's a shame Mischief doesn't like you," Ginger observed with a smile that did weird things to his heart rate.

"And she's such a shy little creature," Justin agreed. "So inhibited." Laughing together eased the momentary paralysis that seemed to have hit his brain.

Ginger found it hard to keep her wits about her. This tall, handsomely dressed man-about-town was definitely not the Justin she'd met yesterday. The midnight-blue suit beneath his elegant overcoat was superbly tailored, accenting his lean hips and broad shoulders, while the pale blue shirt and red-and-grey tie drew her eyes to his face.

What had changed about him? His features were still rough-cut, the high cheekbones giving a slight tilt to his storm-cloud eyes. His square chin jutted stubbornly and his mouth ... She forced herself to look away from his lips as they softened under her gaze. How come she hadn't remembered he had such a seductive mouth? And why did she find it so fascinating?

"So how is Dena feeling?" Justin asked as he held her coat for her, managing to casually brush the curls on the nape of her neck. Her hair was just as enticingly soft as it looked. He wanted to bury his fingers in it.

The mention of her aunt broke through her odd fascination with this new Justin, enabling her to concentrate on something besides his disturbing physical presence. "I'm worried about her," she admitted.

"Is her hip worse?" His immediate concern reminded her of how close he and her aunt seemed to have become. Even in Willow Run, a person didn't ask just anyone to check on the dog.

She forced the speculative thoughts away, focusing on the more immediate problem. "No, her hip seems to be progressing nicely. It's this Willow Run Inn thing that has me worried. She's so excited about all her plans that I hate to discourage her, but it sounds to me like it could turn into a financial disaster."

Now why had she confided that to Justin? Her aunt's investments were none of his business. She, of all people, should know that real estate ventures could be ruined by too much talk. But she did need to discuss Dena's latest dream with someone and, according to Sandy, Justin had single-handedly revived his family furniture factory. Also, he would know the ins and outs of the local business scene, which was something she had to consider. Besides, she really wanted his opinion.

"Risky maybe, but a disaster? Why?" Justin frowned as he opened the car door for her. "Didn't she tell you her plans? I thought it sounded like it could be a real winner both for her and for the town." He was grateful to have something concrete to focus on—his strong physical reaction to Ginger had him feeling slightly disoriented and he definitely wasn't ready to handle any emotional involvement.

"If it works, I suppose that's true, but who is going to handle all the complex details that have to be taken care of?

This is no small project she can dabble with, Justin. It's going to be a major headache for a long time and I'm not sure she's up to it.'' Ginger stared at the passing street as she voiced her deepest fears.

"So what do you think she should do, just forget it?" Disapproval gave his question an edge. "Or don't you think she's smart enough to handle something this big?"

"Aunt Dena's smart enough, but she's in the hospital with a broken hip, Justin. How do we know she'll ever be up to..." Guilt stopped her. Her pessimistic assessment sounded suspiciously like what her mother had said when she'd called about Dena's accident—a truly frightening realization.

She wanted to share Justin's belief in Dena's plan, but what if he was wrong? What if Dena's newest project ended up destroying everything Dena had here?

Ginger's negative tone rubbed over Justin like sandpaper. "I thought that was why you were here, Ginger—to help Dena until she could handle the project on her own."

"How can I help her when I don't know the details of the project? I haven't even seen the inn in nearly ten years and what I remember wasn't very promising." Anger rescued her from depression. Who did he think he was, making it sound as if she was letting Dena down by trying to be practical?

"Depends on how you look at it." Justin felt the chill growing between them and wondered what he'd said to set her off. Maybe talking about Dena wasn't such a good idea, but he couldn't just let it go. He'd been with Dena when she'd checked out the old inn before she signed the papers, and she'd made him see it in a whole new way.

"How do you look at it?" Ginger forced away her guilt and anger. She wasn't going to be like Mom, always making snap judgments about people and their dreams, then defending them even after she was proved wrong. Besides, she wanted to be wrong in her assessment of Dena's project.

"Why don't I explain tomorrow morning while we look the place over?" Justin slowed as he made the turn into the street that led up to the Candlelight Supper Club, which was located on a ridge above town. "I mean, it's too dark for you to really appreciate the details tonight."

"I couldn't ask . . ." Ginger trailed off as Justin glared at her. She was doing it again. Why couldn't she just accept Justin's offer as she would have accepted the same suggestion from a stranger? She grinned at him. "Thank you, I would appreciate your showing me around, Justin, if you can spare the time."

"I'm the boss, so who's going to dock my pay?" He met her gaze and once again felt that odd sensation of heat and chill in his belly. "Besides, tomorrow's Saturday."

"So it is. I've sort of lost track of the days, being away from the office, I mean." She had a little trouble remembering exactly how to breathe when his gaze sent shivers down her spine. Could it be the altitude? Some kind of weird mountain madness? That made more sense than believing that she was attracted to Justin McGovern.

"I suppose you miss running your company." He parked beside the rustic, two-story log building. "Working with real estate in the Los Angeles area must be a real challenge." This was not a subject he wanted to talk about, but it made sense for him to keep her other life in mind, considering the way she seemed to affect him.

"It has its moments, all right." Ginger slipped out of the car immediately. She definitely didn't want to talk about California now.

Justin took her arm as they crossed the rutted parking lot. Western swing music blared around them even before Justin opened the door. It looked just as she remembered. The entry was wide, offering a couple of benches and a small fireplace as well as an ornamental cashier's cage. Straight ahead and up a half-dozen steps an authentic-looking pole gate stood open to give access to the Old-West-style bar and dance floor area, while carpeted stairs led down to the huge lower-level dining room.

"I made our dinner reservation for eight. I hope that's all right. I thought we could have a couple of drinks and enjoy the music before we go downstairs," Justin explained as they stepped past the gate into a deafening blast of music.

Ginger cringed slightly from the sound and from the on-slaught of curious stares that greeted them. Somehow in her fantasies she'd overlooked the fact that everyone in the place would know Justin and a good share of them would re-member her. The realization that by morning everyone in Willow Run would know about their date surrounded her like a black cloud.

"Is something wrong?" Justin sensed Ginger's change of mood. He led her toward the gathering of tables and booths that spread out from the bar. It seemed to take forever to reach an unoccupied table.

"Culture shock." Ginger sank into a chair, wishing mightily for a dark corner to hide in.

"I suppose this isn't the kind of place you're used to." Justin felt the chasm widening between them. Bringing her here had definitely been a mistake. "I forgot that California entertaining is usually done at cocktail parties or the country club."

She didn't miss the sarcasm in his tone and it rankled. "Actually, I rarely entertain except for business, and when we have clients to impress, a quiet restaurant or a private club is quite effective."

"We?" Justin zeroed in on the word.

"My partner and I." Ginger met his frown with one of her own. What the heck had happened to the easygoing Justin? Maybe dressing up made him touchy. "That's why

I was free to come and help Dena. Les can keep things going while I'm here.''

"Oh.'' Les, huh. Somehow he'd hoped for a female partner. So, was this guy a working partner or a special friend? Justin glared around the room, pretending to look for the cocktail waitress while he regained his composure.

Why did he care about Ginger's personal life? What business was it of his, anyway? A casual dinner between old friends didn't entitle him to the details of her love life. After all, this wasn't a real date—was it? He managed a polite smile as he turned back and inquired about her drink preference.

Ginger studied him, trying hard to figure out what had happened. She'd felt close to him in the car while they were discussing Dena, but now... Had her change of mood somehow insulted him? Maybe she'd given him the impression that she thought she was too good for the Candlelight. She sighed, aware there was only one way to find out.

The moment the cocktail waitress left to get their drinks, she gave him her best smile. "I'm so happy you brought me here, Justin. A date to the Candlelight was one of my favorite teenage fantasies.''

"And now it gives you culture shock?'' He couldn't quite keep the sarcasm out of his voice. Her pleasant words didn't mean a thing except that she was trying to smooth over her reaction to the place.

Ginger controlled an urge to grind her teeth in frustration. Obviously, he wasn't going to make this easy for her. "It's not the place, Justin, it's my reaction to it. Do you realize that tonight is the first time in ten years that I've walked into a nightclub that wasn't full of strangers? I guess it kind of overwhelmed me to realize that I used to consider most of these people my friends.''

Was she for real? Justin met her gaze, trying to see beyond her public mask to the girl he'd known so long ago.

Her hazel eyes, so intriguingly flecked with gold and green, seemed open and honest, but how could he be sure? Again he refused to ask himself why it was so important. "How about a dance—think that might make you feel more at home?"

"Sounds good to me." Relief at the softening she could see in his face added enthusiasm to her acceptance. If dancing would put them back on a friendly footing, she was more than willing to try it. "I just hope your toes are up to this," she murmured, as they stepped onto the dance floor. "I can't remember the last time I danced."

"Darn, I left my steel-toed boots at home, too." Justin took her in his arms as the band cooperatively switched to a romantic ballad about finding lost love and mending broken dreams.

Ginger's chuckle turned breathless as Justin's gentle embrace set off a quivering deep inside her and her heart began to pound. Since when had a waltz become an aerobic exercise? The musky scent of his after-shave made her so dizzy she had to fight an urge to rest her cheek against his shoulder.

Justin realized his mistake immediately. Holding Ginger in his arms did nothing to clear up his mental confusion. But oh, it felt wonderful. She moved with him as though they'd been dancing together for years and when she looked up at him, her mask had vanished and he could see a vulnerable innocence that was totally at odds with the sophisticated woman he knew her to be. He ached to draw her closer and explore the possibilities her soft lips seemed to offer.

Ginger was relieved when the band switched to a much faster beat. Cuddling in Justin's arms was just too tempting. Still, she resented it when one of the men from the bar, who'd been a classmate in high school, cut in. Justin reclaimed her soon enough, but they were quickly interrupted by another old friend. And so it continued, no one giving her time to catch her breath, until the band announced it was taking a break.

"I think I might enjoy one of those nightclubs where we didn't know anyone," Justin teased as they collapsed at their table. "I feel like I'm fighting off half the male population of Willow Run every time I want another dance."

"Justin, you didn't tell me Ginger was in town." More old friends arrived at the table, pulling up chairs and filling the air with questions and shared memories.

At first Ginger resented the intrusions, then she forced herself to relax. She should be grateful to all of them, she told herself sternly; they were probably saving her from making a total idiot of herself. The sensations she'd felt those first few moments in Justin's arms were far better left unexplored. She'd already proven once too often that she couldn't handle relationships, so she shouldn't inflict her crazy longings on a nice guy like Justin.

After more dancing and reminiscing, Ginger was relieved when the waitress came to tell them that their table in the dining room was waiting. She'd had more than enough of the music, smoke and noise. Now she craved some uninterrupted time to talk with Justin.

"Ah, alone at last," Justin intoned as they started down the second staircase to the dining room. "I should have known better than to bring the local celebrity here on a Friday night."

"Local celebrity—me?" Ginger giggled. "Come on."

"Hey, you're a success story, lady. You went to the big city and made good all on your own." And he'd better remember it, Justin told himself. All the teasing and laughing in the bar had made him feel closer to Ginger, but now it was time to sober up emotionally.

"So what? You made good here in Willow Run. Dena was telling me all about your innovative new designs and increased sales. You didn't tell me that your furniture is being featured by several interior decorators in Denver.'' Ginger looked up at him, her attention caught by the square strength of his jaw and the wayward lock of midnight hair that was curling around his ear. It took all her self-control to keep from reaching up to smooth it back.

Ginger shook her head, shocked by her longing to touch him. Where was that coming from? Too much wine, maybe? She wanted to believe that, but a little voice deep inside reminded her that she had only had a couple of glasses and it had never affected her that way before. So maybe she was just hungry.

The dining room was large and even though most tables were filled it seemed uncrowded as they were escorted to a table for two in front of the broad window that overlooked the valley. Ginger gasped in delight at the magnificent view.

Though darkness had fallen long ago, the moon rode high and reflected brightly on the snow, deepening the shadows that marked the forested flanks of the mountains. Lights twinkled merrily in the town below and from a dozen outlying areas.

"Looks pretty from up here, doesn't it?" Justin rested his hands on her shoulders, his thumbs gently stroking the back of her neck as he stood behind her at the window. "If it was daylight, you'd be able to see the inn from here and once it's all lit and running . . ."

"Do you really think it could be successfully opened again?" She didn't bother to hide the longing she felt.

"Wait till you hear all Dena's plans for the place. When she showed me around, I could almost see how it was going to look."

"She told you all about it?" Her interest in the scene below faded as she tried to absorb this new information. When had her aunt become so close to Justin and why?

"She came and talked to me just before she signed the final papers. I think she wanted a man's perspective on the deal before she committed herself. Besides, she knew that Mom's family once owned the inn and I think she hoped I could help with some background on the property." Justin was sorry when Ginger turned from the window and allowed him to seat her at the table. He'd felt something special flowing between them for a moment, but now she was all business again.

"I didn't know your family had owned the inn."

"No reason why you should—it was a long time ago. My great-grandfather built it, but my grandfather lost his money and had to sell the place. According to Mom, that's when the inn started going downhill, but that could be sour grapes. I do know she loved it. We used to spend a lot of Sundays picnicking in the area. Maybe that's why I'm so glad Dena is going to keep it from being destroyed."

"Let's hope that's how it works out." Ginger felt hollow as her doubts returned. What if Justin's enthusiasm for the project was rooted in his own romantic notions about rebuilding a family dream? If only she were in California where she could call on her friends in the real estate development business and ask their opinions. This really wasn't her area of expertise and she hated risking Dena's future on just her own opinion.

Justin sighed, wishing he'd never mentioned the inn. This was supposed to be their evening to have fun and he definitely didn't want to waste it talking business. They'd been having such a good time earlier, he'd hoped to continue the magic once they were alone.

Which showed just what kind of a fool he was. This whole evening was nothing more than an attempt to recreate something that had never happened anywhere except in his daydreams. The Ginger he'd had a crush on didn't exist any longer and he'd better accept that before he got in too deep.

Ginger watched his face, seeing the warmth fade as her lack of enthusiasm reached him. She was doing it again.

Raining on Justin's parade just the way she had on Dena's. When had she started sounding so much like her mother? Was it just since her arrival here?

Vowing to erase his frown, Ginger produced a smile as she reached across the table to touch Justin's hand. "What do you say we forget about the inn and all that business for tonight? I can't make any decision until I've had a chance to see it and worrying about it doesn't help."

Her touch was cool, yet when he turned his hand to lace his fingers with hers, he could feel the heat pulsing through him. He lifted her hand to his face, rubbing her silky skin lightly along his jaw. What would she do if he kissed her fingers, tasted them? The waitress arrived before he could find out.

Time for sanity, Justin told himself as the waitress left with their order. This might be a first date, but they weren't carefree teenagers with only themselves to consider and he'd better not forget it. "So, tell me more about your company, your life in Seaview."

Ginger accepted the safe topic happily. She was proud of her success in the property management business and the life-style she'd made for herself. Yet even as she described it, she couldn't help noticing a few hollow spots in her world. She was busy and successful, but she was alone. No one in California would be missing her tonight.

Justin listened closely, not just to her words, but to her tone. She loved her company, that was obvious, but what about the rest of her life? She said little about her partner, Les, and nothing at all about romantic attachments. He didn't know whether to be encouraged or suspicious. Mostly he was just confused.

Still, being with her was terrific fun. As they ate, they found a million things to laugh about and later, when they went back upstairs, they danced contentedly until the band quit for the night.

Ginger stretched and yawned as Justin parked in front of her aunt's house. "I had a wonderful time tonight," she murmured, shivering as she stepped out into the cold night air. Now that she'd discovered the magic of his company, she hated to return to the real world where people had to plan ahead and think about the consequences of their actions.

"It was special," Justin agreed, "but tomorrow is going to be a busy day." He followed her to the front door, waited as she fumbled for Dena's keys, then unlocked the door for her. When she smiled her thanks up at him, he ached to kiss her, but the outside world was already intruding in the form of Mischief, barking loudly on the other side of the door.

He groaned. "I'd better be on my way before that mutt rouses the neighborhood. What time do you want me to pick you up in the morning?" He ordered his feet to move away, but he seemed rooted to the spot.

"Not too early." Ginger closed her eyes, not wanting to think about tomorrow. Tonight was too pleasant to ruin with reality.

"Ten, okay?" Her mouth looked so soft, so inviting, all he had to do was... Mischief's barking escalated and he forced himself to turn away. Better not to kiss her, not to taste her sweet lips. He had a strong hunch that one kiss would never be enough and that scared the hell out of him.

Chapter Four

Feeling abandoned, Ginger stepped inside and picked up the overenthusiastic dog before she could shred her stockings. She gently shook her. "You are a noisy beast, Mischief. I'm surprised nobody calls the cops to complain."

A pink tongue caught the tip of her nose just as Justin's car roared to life. Mischief snuggled into her arms, obviously confident that Ginger really was glad to see her. Ginger sighed, confusion swirling through her disappointment now that he was gone.

What the heck had happened out on the front porch? Why hadn't Justin kissed her? There'd been a moment when she'd been so sure that he wanted to, then suddenly he'd just turned and walked away without a backward glance.

Had she said something, done something to turn him off? She tried to think, but she was too weary to make sense of anything that had happened. She'd think about it tomorrow, she decided. Her spirits lifted a little as she remembered that she'd be seeing Justin tomorrow, too.

Not to mention the infamous Willow Run Inn, she reminded herself, setting the dog down and shrugging out of
her coat. The weight of the evaluation she was going to have
to make settled about her shoulders, banishing the magic
left over from her evening with Justin. This was no time for
errant hormones. If she didn't keep her wits about her tomorrow, Dena could end up being the one hurt.

Thanks to a restless night, Ginger was ready long before
Justin arrived at ten. Since the day was both gloomy and
cold, she fixed a thermos of coffee and borrowed Dena's
bright blue ski jacket, white knit cap and mittens, as well as
her snow boots.

"Hey, you look almost like a native," Justin teased when
she stepped out on the porch with the excited schnauzer.

"I was a native." Her firm resolve about keeping her
mind on business teetered precariously as he grinned at her.
"I hope you don't mind taking Mischief," she murmured,
trying to ignore the odd sensations that spread like lava
through her veins. "She gets so bored at home."

"I was going to suggest it." Justin took both the thermos
and leash as Mischief threatened to pull Ginger off the porch
into the snow. "She loves to go in the car. Dena takes her
everywhere."

"You and Dena are pretty good friends, aren't you?" Her
curiosity surfaced again.

"She gave me a lot of good advice after Mom died. Holly
and Michael weren't all that thrilled to have big brother
running their lives and Dena...well, she could talk to them
and to me, help us work things out." He looked embarrassed. "She sort of got me though my grief, too, so I could
help the kids."

"That must have been a terrible time for you." She could
see the remembered pain in his face as he spoke, but it was
the gentleness of his expression that really touched her. She

knew about grief from when she'd lost her father, but she hadn't been able to handle it with kindness or caring for anyone else. In her feeling of abandonment, she'd lashed out at everyone, including Dena. "I guess Aunt Dena learned all about handling unhappy teenagers from me," she admitted as they got in the car.

"As I recall, you were a bit of a handful, but you turned out fine." His imitation of Dena's familiar words and tone made her laugh in spite of the painful memories.

"I'm not sure she always felt it was worth the battle, but maybe now I can make up for all the times I made her life miserable." That was why she was here, she reminded herself firmly, settling the dog on her lap and looking out the window. "So let's see what the inn has to offer."

"I think all that really matters to Dena is that you came when she needed you. She's been pretty lonesome since she lost her husband two years ago. That's why she got Mischief and probably what made this project so attractive to her. She's not a lady who's meant for quiet retirement." There was admiration in Justin's voice.

"I know she was always involved in Uncle Ben's business, but I didn't realize..." Ginger let it trail off, embarrassed to discover just how little she did know about her aunt. All these years she'd loved Dena, but she'd never really understood her. It was scary.

"Hey, that's nothing to frown about. You're going to love her plans for the inn. It's a real estate developer's dream."

Ginger winced. "The last person I heard say that is now in a California jail for land fraud."

"Ah, but this is Colorado and everybody here is interested in making things better in Willow Run."

"Everybody as in who?" She turned to look at him, sensing that he was serious. "Have you been talking to people about this?"

"The subject has come up pretty often. Half the town knew that Dena bought the land out from under the condo people and they're all anxious to know what she's going to do. Anything that brings in tourist business is going to affect just about everybody in town."

His words had a positive sound, but she sensed that there was more that he wasn't telling her. "How do people feel? Are they as excited about the project as Dena?"

He slowed and looked her way for a moment, his expression unreadable. "About half and half."

"Half and half what?" She felt a chill that had nothing to do with the outside temperature.

"Half interested in seeing Dena develop the inn and half ready to kill her for scuttling the condo deal."

"They wanted the condos?" This was the first she'd heard of that possibility.

"Condos would have brought tourist dollars to most of the local businesses and, of course, there would have been jobs while they were being built." He sighed. "Things can be pretty rough in a small town, Ginger. Remember how anxious we were to leave? Well, things haven't changed too much, except that now the kids don't really have a choice. There just aren't many jobs here."

"Your factory...?"

"We've expanded some and probably will again if the orders keep coming in, but most of my people started with Mom. It's just that now I can give them steady work year-round instead of having to lay them off when things are slow. Not every place is booming like California."

"And you really think the Willow Run Inn could change things here?" She couldn't help being skeptical. "What if no one comes?"

"Crestline is already overcrowded from the Snow Shadow ski development, so there's a good chance we could pick up their fallout. And a lot of people do drive through here in the summer." He shrugged as he turned off the highway. "You know real estate well enough to know there are no guarantees, but with a lot of work and a little luck ..."

"A lot of luck." Ginger peered out at the shadowed tunnel that led beneath the spreading firs. "Not to mention a new road."

The car wallowed in the drifts of snow, but Justin held it in the track easily enough. "Come on, think like a tourist. This is a rustic and romantic old country inn hidden away from the world."

"I could use you to do my advertising copy in Seaview. ' She tried for cynicism, but something about his description had slipped through her defenses. She felt a thrill of anticipation as they made the final turn and emerged on the crest of the little ridge where his family had built the imposing timber-and-stone building.

"Well, here we are." Justin stopped a few yards from the weathered gray stone walls, parking in a spot the wind had swept nearly free of snow.

Ginger swallowed hard as she got out of the car. She'd forgotten just how big the inn was. The beautiful stone walls rose about ten feet, then a second floor had been constructed from sturdy logs cut in these very mountains. "Bulldozing that wouldn't have been easy," she murmured, struck by just how solid and indestructible it looked.

"It would have been criminal." Justin laughed as Mischief forced Ginger into his arms by wrapping her leash around them as she raced in circles. He reluctantly set the dog free.

Ginger stayed nestled in his arms for a moment before she forced her mind back to more practical matters. "Mischief won't get lost, will she? Dena'd kill me."

"She's real good." Justin whistled and the schnauzer came bounding back. "We'll take her in with us, just to be on the safe side."

"Inside?" Ginger eyed the large padlock that secured the thick-paneled double doors that dominated the porch, which was slightly recessed beneath the overhang of the second story. "I didn't think to ask Dena for the keys."

"No problem." Justin headed for the deep-set window to the right of the door. "The spare is here somewhere." He tugged at several of the stones in the sill until one moved and exposed a key. He unlocked the door. It opened with an appropriately eerie creak.

"I hope you remembered a flashlight." Ginger shivered as she peered into the yawning darkness, her enthusiasm for exploring fading fast.

"Don't need it." Justin picked up a lantern, shook it, then dug out a match and lit it. "All the comforts of home."

"Only if you lived here a hundred years ago." Ginger closed the door behind Mischief, then watched as the dog raced across the room, nose to the floor. "What do you suppose she's trailing?"

"Probably a field mouse. They tend to move inside when it gets cold."

"Terrific. No lights and varmints. This is not the home I had in mind." She didn't want this responsibility. She longed to escape back to California and let Dena and Justin work out the project. They both seemed able to see possibilities here that totally escaped her.

"Come on, grumpy, look around. It's not that bad. Dena had the wiring and the plumbing checked out and it's in surprisingly good shape. Pete Green and Miles Vincent both told her that they could have the place operational for a reasonable cash outlay." He lifted the lantern high so that the warm light drove back the shadows and exposed the handsome proportions of the room.

"Well, at least that's good news," she conceded. The huge stone fireplace built into the side wall drew her eyes and she suddenly found herself picturing people gathered before it on a winter evening, talking and enjoying the roaring fire. And in the summer, this room would be filled with the sweet scent of pine and flowers as breezes swept through the generous windows.

Her imagination caught fire. There was plenty of space for a desk opposite the door and with a number of furniture groupings, the room would welcome guests like a spacious living room. Of course they'd need colorful Indian blankets and wall hangings to brighten the stone walls and imaginative lighting, but with the right touches the place could be very special.

"Dena thought of having old-fashioned furnishings throughout—keep the twentieth century at bay as much as possible without sacrificing modern convenience. The attic here is full of furniture and most of it looks to be in pretty good shape—probably just replaced during one of the changes of ownership. I told her we could handle anything that needs repair or reupholstering. I've got a couple of employees who can work wonders, mostly because that's what they did during the times they were laid off from the factory."

"So let's get on with the tour." Ginger tried to match his enthusiasm. "How's the kitchen?"

It was nearly noon by the time they finally returned to the main room. "Why don't I go out and get that thermos," Justin suggested. "You look like a lady who needs a break before we finish the tour."

"There's more?" Ginger looked around, wishing that they had some of the chairs or couches she'd seen in the attic. The huge room intimidated her; in fact, the whole building seemed to weigh on her now that Justin had stopped creating his word pictures.

"I thought we could drive to the lake. Dena has plans for improvements there, too." Justin's eyes met hers with a warmth that eased her back into the world of imagination they'd been sharing as they explored. It scared her to realize how quickly she'd come to love that world.

"Sure, why not?" She turned away from him, afraid to surrender again to the magic spell he'd woven as they moved through the rooms of the inn. A chill touched her as she banished the dream images and, shivering, she wrapped her arms around herself. "Darn, I wish we'd started a fire before we went upstairs."

"I was afraid to. I doubt the chimney's been cleaned in years. I'll bring in a couple of blankets. We can sit on one and wrap up in the other." He chuckled. "Might even be more fun than a fire." He went out, closing the door behind him.

Ginger caught her breath as a flash of heat coursed through her, easily banishing the chill of the abandoned building. What was happening to her imagination? Everything Justin said seemed to fill her mind with pictures, which was fine when he was telling her about Dena's plans for the inn. But the images filling her mind now had nothing to do with Dena. And her response made it clear that she'd better get her self-control in gear now, while she still could.

But how? She couldn't exactly run away from Justin, not when he was being so kind and helpful . . . not to mention charming and intriguing and . . . Ginger swore at herself, then banished her wayward thoughts as a flurry of barking erupted from the rear of the building.

"Mischief! Here, girl." She called twice, even tried whistling, which she didn't do nearly as well as Justin. The barking just grew louder and more insistent. Well aware that the windows in the back of the inn were boarded over, she picked up the lantern and hurried off to investigate.

She found Mischief digging madly at the scarred wood of a tall old corner cabinet. "Cut it out, dog," she ordered, setting the lantern on the sink so she could grab the dog's collar and pull her away. "If you've chased a mouse in there, let it alone."

The schnauzer gave her an outraged look, then jerked free as she leaped forward for another attack. The cabinet rocked under the force of her paws. "Come on, dog, you're going to splinter that door." Ginger reached for the dog again, but Mischief dodged away, her barking forgotten for the moment.

In that brief silence, Ginger heard it. Something was moving inside the cabinet, moving and growling. A shiver of fear traced down her spine. Mischief plunged at the cabinet again, setting it to rocking even more. Fearing the dog would free whatever animal was inside, Ginger made another grab for Mischief, this time snatching her off her feet.

"What the hell?" Justin's voice brought her head around as she hugged the struggling dog to her chest.

Before she could answer or explain, he came racing across the worn kitchen tile to collide with her, knocking her to the floor just as the cabinet rocked forward, spilling a large black object from the top. It crashed to the floor with a force that seemed to shake the entire building.

The cabinet door burst open and Mischief yelped and tried to leap free as Justin's heavy weight settled protectively over Ginger. "Hold her," he shouted as a furry shape flashed by and disappeared into a black hole half hidden behind the stove. "If she gets in there, we'll never get her out."

Ginger kept her death grip on Mischief as she tried to catch her breath. "What was that?" she gasped when she could finally speak.

"I don't know, but it was too big to be a rat." Justin eased himself off her, grinning. "Just be grateful it wasn't a skunk." He took the struggling dog out of her arms. "You okay?"

Ginger sat up slowly, feeling a few pangs from her muscles as she looked around. The cabinet door had splintered, but what sent a chill through her was the heavy black iron bootjack that now lay approximately where she and Mischief had been standing. "I—I didn't know that was up there."

Justin set Mischief in her lap, then picked up the bootjack, grunting under the weight of it. He set it down in front of the hole, effectively blocking it. "I saw it from the door. The cabinet was rocking and it was sliding forward. I thought for a moment..." His voice broke as he held out a hand to her. "You and that dog keep getting into trouble."

His strong, warm fingers closed around hers as she let Mischief go and scrambled to her feet. When she looked into his eyes, she no longer felt the various bumps and bruises. Never before had she known what it meant to be lost in someone's eyes, but now the rest of the world seemed to just fade away.

"If you hadn't come in..." She let it trail off as he released her hand and slipped his arms around her. His gaze moved over her face as though seeking reassurance that she was all right, then his eyes focused on her mouth. Her lips suddenly felt so dry she had to lick them.

She could feel the heat of his hand on her back as he gently traced a finger down her cheek then slowly drew it along her lower lip. His hand was shaking slightly, but then, so was she. Her heart rate leaped and her knees seemed to weaken as Justin bent his head to hers. Warning bells sounded deep within her, but somehow she found it hard to care as she lifted her lips to meet his, her eyes drifting shut in anticipation.

His mouth brushed hers gently, teasing, caressing like a summer breeze, as his arm tightened, drawing her closer against the hard length of him. His fingers tangled in the thickness of her hair, holding her head steady as he took command of her mouth. Shivers of heat traced through her as her lips parted in welcome and she surrendered to the myriad of new sensations that his touch unleashed.

Without thought, she wound her arms around him, clinging to him, caressing his back with one hand while the other found the nape of his neck. Never had she been so deeply aware of another human being or as little interested in anything else around her. She never wanted the moment to end... or reality to return.

Justin felt the heat that flowed from their eager mouths to burn deep within him. Ginger's response stunned him. She seemed to welcome his kiss, clinging to him with the same aching hunger that pulsed through him. He tasted the sweetness of her mouth, closing his mind against the small voice that shouted that he must stop before it was too late.

Even with his eyes closed he could see the teetering boot-jack and Ginger below it reaching for the dog. He deepened the kiss, reassuring himself that she was safe and here in his arms. She belonged here, she felt so right, she...

Shock pushed back the drugging sensations and allowed sanity to flow back into his brain. He slowly became aware of more than the soft contours of the woman in his arms—of Ginger. He heard Mischief's whining and scratching and the creaking of the building as it warmed in the sun that had finally broken through the clouds. Unwilling to fully break the wondrous contact, he rained kisses from the corner of her mouth along her jaw, ending at the tender spot just below her ear.

What was she doing? Ginger stiffened as Justin's lips left hers. What kind of madness had taken hold of her? She loosened her death grip on his shoulders and took a shaky breath, hoping that it would clear her foggy mind. So he'd probably saved her life—that was no reason to throw herself at him and... And enjoy herself so completely in the process.

Sensing Ginger's change of mood, Justin stepped back, hiding his reluctance with a slightly shaky grin. "Ready for our coffee break?"

"Coffee?" Ginger looked around, trying to focus her eyes as well as her mind. Her head was still spinning, though she couldn't be sure whether it was from contact with the floor or the impact of Justin's kiss. "Oh, the thermos."

"I dropped it in the main room when I heard the ruckus out here." Justin turned away to scoop up the frustrated dog, who was still trying to pry the bootjack away from the hole it covered.

Ginger took another deep breath, telling herself firmly that she was not disappointed at Justin's casual dismissal of what had just happened between them. She was grateful that he was being so... calm about it. After all, neither of them had any interest in pursuing what had been simply a moment of weakness.

So why did she feel abandoned? Why did she want to take Mischief's place in Justin's arms? Her mountain-madness theory seemed a little weak to cover what she'd just experienced, but she was afraid to consider any other explanation. She couldn't be so wildly attracted to Justin McGovern—not after all these years.

"I'll nail a board over that hole before we leave." Justin closed the kitchen door. "That will keep the critter out of the building, anyway."

"By trapping it in the cellar?"

"I doubt it. Likely there are a couple of broken boards in the outside doors. That's probably how it got in. Of course, we could always take the mighty hunter down there and turn her loose to find out."

"Thanks, but I've had just about enough excitement for one day." Ginger met his gaze and felt her heart rate accelerate. More than enough excitement, she told herself firmly, and not all of it had been caused by Mischief.

Justin chuckled. "City girl. If you're going to help Dena out with this place, you're going to have to make peace with the local residents."

Her momentary joy in just being close to him faded away. "That's a pretty big if, Justin."

"You can't see how terrific this place could be?" He sounded disappointed as he retrieved the abandoned blankets and thermos, then produced a dented box of doughnuts. "I thought you were really getting in the mood when you came up with all those ideas for redoing the rooms upstairs."

"Oh, I can see it all right," Ginger admitted as she shook out one of the blankets and spread it in the small patch of sunshine that came in through a partially unboarded window. "I'm just not convinced that Dena is going to be able to create this resort. It's a little more than renovation and redecorating. She's going to need a commitment from the community—help both in financing the project and in the related facilities."

"Like what?"

"To begin with, someone to plan and build the boat dock at the lake—a person who'll supply the equipment and actually operate the concession there on a share basis. And the same goes for the cross-country skiing part of the enterprise. That's a major project itself—one that requires someone who can lay out trails, arrange for rental equipment and offer instruction. The Willow Run Inn will need to offer attractions in both summer and winter to make it pay off, and Dena's going to have her hands full just running the place."

Ginger was delighted to discover that her pulse rate stayed normal even when Justin sat down on the blanket beside her. Reality therapy seemed to be working—except for a sudden warmth that spread through her when his hand brushed her cheek as he settled the second blanket over her shoulders. The heat increased as he moved closer to her, sharing the blanket.

"Sounds like you do have a handle on the project," he observed, opening the doughnuts while she poured the coffee. "Do you think Dena has people in mind for those concessions?"

"I haven't had time to ask her." Ginger helped herself to a doughnut, then laughed as Mischief suddenly turned away from her prowling to come running. "Tired of hunting your food, dog?" she asked as Mischief sniffed the box.

"Can't blame her for preferring a meal that doesn't run away." Justin offered the dog a small bite. "Besides, my pushing you out of the way cheated her out of her prey in the kitchen."

Ginger sighed. "You also saved both of us from being flattened. I really do thank you for the rescue."

"Sorry it had to be so rough." He touched the side of her face lightly. "I sure didn't mean to bruise you."

It took all her self-control not to press her cheek against his warm fingers, to perhaps turn her head and kiss the palm of his hand. The idea was so attractive she ached with denial even as she tried to distract herself from such seductive thoughts. "I'm just grateful and a little worried."

"Worried? Why?"

"I've been here less than three days and you've rescued me twice—first from freezing in a snowdrift, now from a lethal bootjack. Do you think maybe I'm not suited for life in the wild mountains?" She tried to keep her tone light, but an odd quiver seemed to come into her voice. Deep down she was afraid, not of the snow or the falling bootjack, but of what she felt every time Justin touched her.

"Well, I suppose it could be a problem," Justin answered, frowning at her. "Luckily, there is a simple solution."

"There is?"

"All you have to do is keep me within rescuing distance. I'm sure that you'll get your mountain legs pretty soon and then you'll be able to handle anything that comes along."

"Right." Anything but the dizzy longing she felt when she looked deep into those sexy gray eyes. Could she have hit her head hard enough to get brain damage?

The rest of the tour passed quickly, though they nearly got stuck in a snowdrift trying to reach Willow Lake. Still, the short hike reminded her of all the picnics she'd had on the banks of the small mountain lake. It was another spot time seemed to have missed, and her head quickly filled with daydreams about spending romantic summer evenings here with Justin. More proof of impending brain rot.

"Now what?" Justin asked as he worked the heavy sedan free of the snow and eased his way back toward the highway.

"Now you take me home and I try to figure out what I'm going to tell Dena when I go to the hospital this afternoon."

"Anything I can help you with?" He'd done his best to keep his mind on something other than the feel of her in his arms, but it wasn't easy.

"Thank you, but you've already done more than enough." She ached to spend the rest of the day with him, but she knew she couldn't think straight with him around.

Her smile seemed genuine, but when he looked into her hazel eyes, he could read nothing of her thoughts. It was as though their kiss had never happened, as though they'd never melted into each other and... He stopped himself firmly. Suppose it hadn't happened for her? Maybe he was reading more into her response than he should. He probably should forget the whole thing.... Ha, fat chance.

"Well, if you need any advice, don't hesitate to call me. I'm one of the locals who wants to be involved in this. I really think it could be good for Willow Run." Justin gave her a polite smile. If she wanted things on a businesslike basis, he'd give her businesslike—even if it killed him.

Ginger parked at the hospital long before she was ready to face her aunt. Solitude hadn't brought the detachment she'd expected. Every time she tried to think logically about the problems involved in the project, memories of everything Justin had told her about the inn intruded—along with Justin's image.

For the first time in her life, she couldn't seem to be objective and that really scared her. She'd built her successful life in Seaview on logic, making her choices carefully, never letting her emotions rule her head and now... The moment she'd driven into Willow Run, she'd slipped back into the old ways, the ones that had never brought her any happiness.

She stared up at the hospital. So what did she do about it? Tell Dena to sell, then go home and pack? A part of her approved the idea, but deep down she knew she could never just abandon her aunt. Dena had been there for her at the worst time in her life. She couldn't walk away from her just because she was afraid of her odd new feelings for Justin.

The way to control her emotions was to face them, she decided. So she was attracted to Justin, big deal. She'd had crushes before. Well, maybe not recently, but she had gone through all the fluttery, crazy stuff with Teddy in college and then two years ago there'd been Jim.... She sighed, realizing that she couldn't even remember Jim's last name.

Still, she had been attracted to both men, hadn't she? How much different could this be? It was just complicated because she'd known Justin most of her life, but that could be a plus. After all, he was sure to remember that she never got seriously involved with anyone.

She got out of the car, suddenly aware that she was back to Sandy's suggestion that she just have a friendly fling while she was in town. It sounded so simple, but when she remembered how she'd felt in Justin's arms, that was a whole lot more complicated.

Sighing, she went inside. She'd think about all that later—right now she had to ask Dena if she'd done any work on the financing end of the development. And, of course, she needed to know about people who might be interested in running the concessions and working on the renovations. That would be important if they were actually going to go ahead with the project.

Of course that would be the first topic under consideration, she decided as she tapped on the door, then pushed it open. Her stomach knotted. It was such a big *if,* since she knew her decision could change both their lives forever.

Chapter Five

Ginger felt the tension the moment she stepped into Dena's room. Her aunt's smile looked forced and the man sitting beside her bed was red faced as he rose to greet Ginger. Dena introduced him as Eugene Bennett, a developer from Crestline, adding, "He's come to talk about the inn property."

"You're not the gentleman who was planning to build condos out there, are you?" Ginger pulled up a chair.

"Oh, no, I'm interested in creating a resort in Willow Run, something that can add to the prestige of Snow Shadow, which is another of our projects." Mr. Bennett appeared relieved to turn his attention to her instead of Dena. "Your aunt mentioned that you work in real estate in California, so you may have heard of our corporation." He produced a card.

"The name is familiar," Ginger admitted, studying the elegant, buff-colored rectangle. Trouble was, she couldn't remember what she'd heard about them. "Tell me, what do you have in mind for the inn area?"

"We plan to incorporate most of Mrs. Palmer's ideas." He directed a smile at Dena. "I think making the resort a year-round facility is an excellent one. Of course, we would work on a larger scale. We'd want a number of cabins in addition to the inn, and we might expand the lake into a water park, if we can acquire the land around it."

So much for her daydreams about spending romantic times at the lake with Justin, Ginger thought, then forced her own regrets away. She couldn't afford to reject Mr. Bennett's offer on a whim, when it could be an easy solution to both Dena's financial problems and her own more personal difficulties. "Then you plan to keep the inn building intact?"

"From what I've seen, it lends a certain air to the area." Mr. Bennett's smile widened. "Of course, our crews would come in and gut the building. We've learned that it's much easier that way. Our surveys have proved that people like the illusion of age, but not the inconvenience."

"Your *crews?*" The knot in her stomach tightened at the idea of men destroying the beautiful old wood that formed the walls and floor of the second story. All the decorating ideas that had filled her mind as she toured the building with Justin returned to haunt her.

"Oh, yes, when Recreation, Inc. takes over a property, we handle everything—clearing the land, building roads, providing staff to run the resort once it's finished. All the people of Willow Run will have to do is sit back and reap the profits after we're finished."

"Clearing the land?" The knot was joined by a chill and Ginger could see the horror in Dena's pale face when she glanced her way.

"Can't build a Recreation, Inc. resort in the middle of a forest, Miss Howard. Now, I'd really like to get this settled today, if we can. I just explained to Mrs. Palmer that I'm prepared to offer her five thousand over the price she paid for the property. She gets out of what could be a bad investment with a tidy profit and we will simply carry out her plans for the area." His smile was oily enough to deep-fry a large cow.

"I told you that I'm not going to make a decision today, Mr. Bennett," Dena stated, her voice firm even though her hand was shaking as she reached for a glass of water. "I've listened to your proposal, now I'd like to discuss it with my niece."

The smile congealed as Mr. Bennett got to his feet. "Why don't I wait outside? Perhaps your niece will want further details after you talk."

Ginger bristled as Dena's shaking increased. She had no trouble picturing this man ripping up the inn with his bare hands. "If I do, I'll get in touch with you next week," she told him firmly.

Though he didn't look happy, Mr. Bennett finally seemed to understand that he was losing points by pressuring her. He murmured polite phrases, then left. The moment the door closed behind him, Ginger hurried to her aunt's bedside. "Are you all right? What in the world did he do to you?"

Dena tried to smile, but she couldn't quite make it. "He made me so angry, Ginger. And what he wants to do—it's all wrong for the inn and for Willow Run. It's even worse than the condos. We can't let him..." Her skin grew even paler and beads of perspiration popped out on her forehead. She seemed to be having difficulty breathing.

Frightened, Ginger punched the call button. "Don't worry about Bennett, Dena, just relax. I'll tell him we aren't selling. We won't let him destroy something as lovely as the inn."

It seemed forever before a nurse arrived, and Ginger didn't feel any better when the nurse immediately summoned Dr. Ellis, then ordered Ginger to wait outside. What was wrong with Dena? Ginger paced the hall. Was there more to her hospitalization than just her broken hip?

Mr. Bennett materialized in front of her on her second trip along the hall. He beamed at her. "Finished with your discussion already, Miss Howard?"

The sight of him turned her worry to anger and he was the perfect target. She straightened to her full five-six and glared at him. "My aunt and I had very little to discuss, Mr. Bennett, since we both found your plans appalling. We definitely aren't interested in your offer, as we plan to develop the site as it should be."

"Yourselves? You and a little old lady who can't even get out of her hospital bed? Fat chance." His smile turned to ice. "All you're doing by being stubborn about selling is cutting the price, Miss Howard. I'll get the property, but by the time I do, you won't be making any profit on the deal, believe me. And don't look for another buyer, either. Once the word is out that Recreation, Inc. is interested, nobody else will be bidding."

"We're not looking for a buyer. I told you, this is our project." Saying the words and seeing Bennett's anger at his defeat felt good, but when he turned and walked away, the chill returned. When had she made her decision? And, more important, how in the world was she going to follow through with it?

Dr. Ellis emerged from Dena's room before she had time to worry about the future. He beckoned to Ginger.

"How is she? What happened?" Ginger had trouble keeping her voice from shaking.

"She's calming down now, but she's got to take it easy for a while, Ginger. Her blood pressure is too high and that developer that just visited her didn't help the situation a bit. Do you think you can keep him away?''

''I've already taken care of that,'' Ginger assured him, wondering as she spoke whether she'd really done Dena a favor by rejecting Bennett's offer. If worry about selling the inn sent her blood pressure up, what would the reality of renovating the property do to her? ''Can I see her?''

''For a few minutes, no longer. I want her to rest, but she's dead set on talking to you and she won't calm down until she does.'' His weary smile showed the depth of his friendship. ''A determined lady, that Dena Palmer.''

''I'll make it brief,'' Ginger promised, well aware that any real discussion of the future was going to have to wait until Dena's blood pressure was under control—and she had the kind of news that would keep it that way.

Ginger drove home slowly, her mind spinning from her few moments with her aunt. Dena had brightened the instant Ginger told her that she'd sent Bennett packing and she'd immediately plunged into her plans for the resort. She'd managed to give Ginger quite a bit to think about before Ginger could convince her that getting some rest was more important than planning for the future of the Willow Run Inn.

Not that she'd be getting any rest, Ginger thought wearily. Now that she'd committed herself to this project, she was going to have to take some action—fast. And she needed help. A smiling face filled her mind as she pulled into the driveway. She'd call Justin. After all, he had pretty much volunteered this morning, so...

Inviting Justin over for an early Sunday dinner was almost too easy. Only after she'd hung up the phone did she wonder if she should ask Robert and Sandy to join them, just so Justin wouldn't get the wrong idea about her being interested in him. She stroked Mischief, who'd curled up in her lap.

"Who am I kidding, dog? I'm afraid he'll get the right idea. A couple more kisses like the one today and I... Well, I'm afraid to guess what might happen. I don't want to hurt him and I sure don't want to get hurt, so somehow, I've got to keep this from getting serious."

Mischief opened one brown eye, peered at her, then yawned and stretched before snuggling more deeply into her lap. Obviously she wasn't worried about the consequences. Sighing, Ginger picked up the phone and called Les. She was surprised to catch him at home on a Saturday afternoon. Taking a deep breath, she warned him that her visit to Willow Run might turn out to be a lot longer than she'd anticipated.

"No problem, Ginger." He sounded disgustingly cheerful. "Take as long as you need. Things are going smooth as silk here. In fact, I think Ann could run the company without either one of us. Have you ever considered offering her a position in the expansion office?"

"Ann?" Ginger frowned as she thought about her secretary. "I didn't realize she'd be interested."

"I don't think she was until yesterday when I started talking about staffing the new office. Of course, I didn't make her an offer or anything, but I definitely got the feeling she would like to move into management. Anyway, it seems to me it would be a lot easier to replace a secretary than to find someone who could run a branch office. What do you think?"

Ginger agreed, then hung up the phone wondering why she felt she'd been away for years instead of days. She was losing control of Howard Management and the company had dominated her world for so long she felt unable to cope with the loss. Deciding not to dwell on it, she slipped out from under Mischief and went to the kitchen to try to figure out what she was going to cook for Justin tomorrow. Though she refused to analyze the reasons, just thinking about Justin lifted her spirits.

By noon on Sunday, Ginger was convinced that yesterday's fall had destroyed her brain. Never a gourmet cook, she couldn't remember exactly which spices went into the sauce for her special chicken and pasta dish, and Dena didn't have the recipe. Guessing left her dubious about the results.

Ginger opened the oven and sniffed. At least it smelled right. Her stomach rumbled in agreement as she turned her attention to the vegetables she planned to cook in the microwave. She'd told him one o'clock, but if he came early...

The shrilling phone interrupted her fuming and she nearly stumbled over Mischief, who obviously agreed about the delicious smell of the cooking chicken. "If he's not coming, I'll kill him," she muttered as she collapsed into the chair.

"Hello, dear." Her mother sounded full of enthusiasm. "How are you this fine day?"

Ginger bit back a groan. Just what she needed—more stress. She did her best to hide her feelings as she answered her mother's questions about Dena's condition and the inn project. Her mother's reaction was exactly what she'd expected.

"Oh, Virginia, how could you let Dena involve you in her nonsense? You've built a wonderful business in California—you don't need the problems you're going to have with that old inn. It never was a success and now... You have to think about your future. If Dena didn't have you to lean on, she'd be much more willing to sell the property."

Ginger couldn't argue with her mother's logic. Yesterday morning, before her tour of the inn, she would have agreed with her evaluation. But something almost magical had happened as she explored the old building with Justin, something that defied logic.

Justin. She smiled as his image filled her mind. For some reason, just thinking about him made it easier to reassure her mother and end the conversation without a disagreement. She even caught herself humming as she returned to the kitchen, no doubt another sign of her failing mental faculties.

Justin checked his watch. Yep, he was going to be early, no doubt a real sin to someone used to entertaining the sophisticated California crowd. Everybody out there probably considered it proper to be fashionably late.

Of course, he shouldn't have accepted her invitation in the first place, he reminded himself. If he had any sense at all, he'd have told her that he had plans for Sunday dinner and spared himself the torment of being near the fiercely independent Miss Howard. But then, he'd never had much resistance where Ginger was concerned, not even in high school. He'd always wanted to ask her out, but back then he hadn't had the guts to risk being turned down.

But she needed him now and so did Dena. Ginger didn't have a hope of making the inn project work without some assistance from the local bankers, and Dena was in no shape to twist arms. Besides, there were the concessionaires to be decided on and all the contracting work and...

He grinned. He was letting himself in for a lot of work, but the idea of sharing it with Ginger made it seem more like fun. Besides, it had been a long time since he'd really felt challenged by a project...or a woman. He pulled up in front of Dena's feeling like an eager seventeen-year-old.

Ginger's heartbeat quickened as Mischief's yelps announced that Justin had arrived. He was early, of course. So why was she grinning like an idiot as she hurried to answer the door? This was just a business luncheon—even if she had spent the whole morning working on it.

Mischief's exuberance eased those first moments, when Ginger looked into Justin's eyes and remembered the mind-blowing kiss they'd shared. Once she'd caught her breath, conversation was easy. Justin had brought some wine and she'd fixed a few hors d'oeuvres so they sipped and munched while she described her visit to the hospital and its dramatic result.

"Then Dena's okay and you're definitely committed to the project?" Justin didn't try to hide his pleasure as he admired the fit of her gold sweater and slacks. "I'm so glad."

"So am I, most of the time." Ginger chuckled. "It's when I start making lists of the things that need to be done that I really wonder about my sanity. I'm not sure I can make it work for Dena and after what happened yesterday, I don't know how much she's going to be able to do."

"Well, it just so happens I'm here to volunteer." Justin reached for another cracker just to keep from touching the bruise on her cheek. Sitting on the couch with her was almost more temptation than he could handle. Unfortunately, after her reaction to yesterday's kiss, he had a strong hunch that she'd take off if he let her know how he felt.

Ginger watched him closely, trying to judge his mood. He was acting like an old friend, but whenever their eyes met, she felt the electricity tingling between them. She definitely didn't want him offering to help for the wrong reason—like wanting a repeat of yesterday's kiss. The flames inside her blazed a little hotter at the memory.

Ginger forced the distracting thoughts away. "Are you sure, Justin? I admit I'm going to need some help, but this really isn't your problem. I'm sure with your factory you have more than enough to worry about."

"You have a business of your own, too." Justin's gaze was unreadable. "Can you afford to stay here while we get things sorted out for Dena?"

"I checked with Les and he seems to think things are going fine without me."

Justin caught the undercurrent of bitterness beneath her light tone. Was it because the business was doing all right without her or because this Les hadn't urged her to hurry back? Something very much like jealousy stabbed at him, making it clear that he wasn't sticking to his resolve to keep this strictly business.

"Then I'm in," he said before he could change his mind. "And I have some suggestions for you." He dug a battered envelope out of his pocket, then grinned at her. "I did some thinking last night."

Ginger started to take it, then lifted her head and sniffed. "Damnation!" She sprinted to the kitchen to snatch the chicken out of the oven.

"Is everything all right?" Justin stopped in the doorway, his look of concern fading as he saw the pan in her hand. "If that's dinner, business can wait. It smells wonderful and I'm starved."

Ginger set the pan down so she could inspect the contents more closely, then sighed with relief. "It's about five minutes from being totally ruined. I forgot to set the timer when you came."

"Well, let's not keep it waiting. What can I do to help?"

"Pour us some more wine while I dish this up." Ginger gave him a grateful smile. "I guess I should have warned you that I'm not the world's best cook."

"Next time we'll pool our talents. I'm not too bad at the basics, thanks to having to cook for the kids part of the time. Holly's getting better, but now that she's going with Phil Durosher, she's not home for too many meals."

Next time. The promise of the words shivered along her nerves. She knew she should say something to derail this feeling that seemed to flare between them, but how could she deny her own longing to see what would come of it? Besides, her brain was so numb she doubted she could come up with a coherent sentence. Maybe she was just too hungry to think.

"Did you say Phil Durosher?" she asked when he returned to the dining room with their glasses and the wine. "Would he be Floyd's younger brother?"

"You remember Floyd?" Justin frowned. Phil's brother was around Ginger's age, but he'd never struck Justin as being a very memorable person. Of course, Justin had left Willow Run after graduation, so maybe Floyd and Ginger...

"Not really. I mean, he was in my class at school, but we weren't close friends. I just recognized the name. Dena said that Floyd had talked to her about the cross-country skiing concession. Seems that Floyd got interested as a Boy Scout and has been trying to get a cross-country skiing club started in Willow Run. I guess Floyd suggested that his brother might be a good possibility for handling the boats."

Justin forgot his momentary jealousy and helped Ginger carry the food into the dining room. "Floyd and Phil, huh? That could be a good combination. I know Phil is worried about the future. He doesn't want to stay on the ranch with his dad and neither does Floyd. Ranching up here is tough and getting worse. They just couldn't figure out anything else to do that would keep them in Willow Run. Like I said, jobs aren't easy to come by."

"Then you think I should approach them?" Ginger relaxed, happy to focus on something besides her wayward emotions. Maybe the secret of keeping things on a friendship basis was just to stay too busy for anything else.

"Why don't you let me sound out Phil first? He spends more time at our house than he does at his own, so I can probably find out how serious he is about the whole thing." He grinned. "I'll even give him a nudge in the right direction. I don't want Holly moving away and I have a hunch if Phil goes, she's going to be right behind him."

"They're that serious? Doesn't she want a career?"

"I tried to talk her into going to college, but she figures she's already got a career with the factory. She's been working there since she graduated from high school."

"Then she likes it?"

"She tolerates it." Justin sighed. "When she first started, I had great hopes for her taking over the business, but now I'm not so sure. She just doesn't seem to grasp the principles of running a business and I'm afraid it's because she really isn't interested."

"Young love can have that effect, or so I've heard."

Her tone had been light, but he couldn't resist the opening she'd given him. "Have you ever been in love, Ginger?"

Ginger nearly choked on her bite of chicken. What the heck had brought that up? And what should she say? She met his gaze, easily reading the intensity of his interest. For some reason he really cared about her answer, so she couldn't evade the question.

"I thought I was a couple of times when I was younger, but nothing ever came of it. After a while, I realized that I wasn't the home-and-family type. Then I got started in real estate management and discovered that I had knack for it, so I decided to forget romance and build a career. I've never been sorry."

Justin winced, wishing he'd thought before he asked. There was something awfully final about her words, kind of like a warning. He didn't like knowing that she was so content with her life. Not that he was surprised—Ginger had never struck him as the kind of woman who needed a man to give her life meaning.

Ginger watched Justin's grin fade and hated herself for being so blunt. But she was just trying to protect him from hurt, she reminded herself. The man was so kind and full of love, he should have someone who could offer him more than just a fling while they worked together. He deserved real love and commitment, two factors of life she'd spent most of her adult years avoiding, and she had no desire to experiment with them now.

Suddenly aware of the silence growing between them, Ginger speared another piece of chicken, then asked, "What about you? Have you ever been in love, Justin?"

Now why had she asked that? Since she wasn't interested, why was she prying into his personal life? She watched his face closely, anxious to hear his answer and already prepared to hate anyone for whom he'd cared deeply.

Justin felt a quick flare of hope at the intensity of Ginger's gaze. She might not realize it, but she cared about his answer just as deeply as he'd cared about hers. What really bothered him was why she seemed so skittish about the subject. If she'd never been in love, why was she so afraid of the emotion?

"I had a couple of brushes with love in college, but none that lasted. Then after I took over the factory, I was too busy to even think about falling in love." He grinned at her. "Guess we both got hooked on our businesses."

"They can take a lot of time and attention." Her throat closed and her heart rate started doing odd things as the warmth of his gaze spread through her. She tried hard for sanity. "And now here we are, planning to take on more work."

Though a part of him ached to press her for more personal conversation, he sensed her withdrawal in the change of subject. Whatever the basis of her insistence on independence, it was obviously going to take some time to convince her that there was more to life than a satisfying career. If he wanted the chance, he was going to have to play by her rules for a while. Resigned to patience, he offered her the envelope again.

Relieved, Ginger plunged enthusiastically into a discussion of possible sources of financing. The scribbled names on the envelope and Justin's promise of support offered her exactly what she needed—hope that they could actually pull this off. Contacting the bankers on her own would be risky, but with Justin beside her and Dena's reputation for good business sense behind her, they'd have to listen with open minds.

They were sipping their after-dinner coffee before they exhausted the subject of the inn's future. Justin, sensing Ginger's good mood, leaned back and patted his lean middle. "That's the best meal I've had in a while, Ginger. I think you underestimate your cooking talents."

Ginger chuckled, basking in his praise and the feeling of companionship. It was amazing how truly comfortable she felt with Justin. "You've tasted my best production, I'm afraid. I also do a passable spaghetti with meatballs, some fairly edible casseroles and a truly inflammable chili. Other than that, I'm pretty good at ordering out or making restaurant reservations."

"Sounds pretty impressive to me. I'm more of a summer cook, myself. I like to grill things. In the winter it's mostly soups and sandwiches or frozen dinners at the McGovern place unless Holly gets the cooking urge. That's one thing about having Phil around—she keeps trying to impress him, so we eat pretty well."

"Having people to cook for makes a difference. Half the time I don't get back to my apartment till late evening, so I just grab a bite whenever it's handy." Or skip dinner entirely, she added to herself, finding thoughts of her California life-style somewhat less than appealing at the moment. She'd never thought of it as lonely before, but maybe that was simply because she'd rarely had time to think about it at all.

"So let's do these dishes, then we can concentrate on our game plan for tomorrow. The sooner we get the ball rolling, the better." He wanted her so deeply involved in the renovations she wouldn't have time to think about or miss her other life. Justin ignored the little voice inside that asked, "Involved with the inn or with you?"

"Oh, don't worry about them. I'll just put everything in the dishwasher." Ginger stacked the dessert plates quickly, feeling awkward at his offer and the closeness it indicated. They could have been an old married couple.

"Okay, I'll rinse, you stack them in." No way was he going to wait in the empty living room while she puttered around in the kitchen. If he could feel the lines of attraction drawing them closer together, so could Ginger and he couldn't let her retreat now.

The kitchen seemed a lot smaller as they moved around it, and every time Justin brushed by her she caught the dizzying scent of his shaving lotion. Her befuddled brain immediately produced memories of being in his arms while they danced and her lips softened, longing for a repeat performance of his heart-stopping kiss. She nearly broke one of Dena's plates in her hurry to escape her own weakness.

Ginger shivered as she stepped into the dim living room. Somehow the day had turned gloomy and cold while they ate and the room reflected it. Or maybe it was her mood; she'd never been able to handle confusion and, thanks to Justin, her emotions were in chaos.

"Would you like me to build a fire?" Justin asked, stepping close behind her to rub her arms with his warm hands.

A nice romantic fire on the hearth sounded wonderful. The chill inside her melted under a burst of heat. "Oh, no need to go to all that trouble,'' she murmured, trying hard to sound convincing.

"What trouble? I'm a country boy, remember?''

She was remembering a lot of things and most of them added to the spreading core of warmth that his touch had ignited. Her will to fight the attraction she felt was weakening with every memory of yesterday's tour of the inn. She settled on the love seat that faced the fireplace and watched as Justin stacked the kindling, lit it, then carefully added several pieces of wood. The sweet scent of burning pine filled the air.

Justin sank down beside her, easing his arm around her shoulders, so that her head rested against his shoulder. ''Now this is my idea of a great way to spend a Sunday afternoon.''

Ginger stiffened her spine for exactly three seconds, then relaxed against him, surrendering to the tender magic of flickering flames and Justin's potent attraction. Justin knew about her other life, the world that she'd have to return to once the inn project was under control. She was aware of his commitment to Willow Run and his family business. If they both knew the score, maybe it wouldn't hurt to just relax and enjoy each other's company while they could. She snuggled against the rough wool of his bright blue sweater. Nothing that felt this right could possibly be a mistake.

As he leaned back against the arm of the love seat, Justin bent his head to touch his lips to the rumpled auburn curls, inhaling the lilac-tinged scent that was so uniquely Ginger. His body responded with an ache of longing, but he ignored his hunger for her. No matter how badly he wanted her, he wasn't going to push for more than she was ready to offer.

Making love to Ginger might be the answer to all his dreams, but he suspected that it would be a nightmare for her, since she seemed afraid of getting too close. Making her vulnerable to her own emotions would probably drive her away faster than anything else. But what would win her? How else could he find the key that would unlock the barriers she'd erected around her heart?

Ginger stirred, no longer content just to recline in his arms. She drew away from him so she could look into his eyes, then used one fingertip to lightly trace the softening contours of his lips. She felt a surge of pleasure as he nipped at her finger, then gently kissed it. His arm tightened around her and his fingers tangled in her hair as his lips descended to claim her willing mouth.

Sparks from the crackling fire seemed to spread into her bloodstream, heating her body as she clung to him, answering his kiss with a joyous longing she'd never felt before. If this was madness, she no longer cared. All she wanted was...

A chill weight landed on her hip and a wet paw dug into her ticklish ribs as Mischief walked up her side. ''Mischief!'' Ginger squeaked as she broke off the kiss. Snowy whiskers touched her cheek as the dog investigated this odd human behavior.

Justin's chest heaved beneath her and his laughter filled the air as he released Ginger to grab their snowy invader, setting Mischief firmly on the floor. ''Dog,'' he groaned, ''you have the worst sense of timing I've ever seen.''

Mischief regarded them both for a moment, then shook, showering them with more melting snow. When neither of them moved, she sighed and settled herself in front of the fire to dry off. Ginger looked up at Justin, then joined his laughter as she relaxed against his broad chest. Mischief might have broken their mood, but she was still in Justin's arms.

Chapter Six

The next hour sped by. They talked and laughed, kissed and cuddled. Ginger felt as though they'd escaped the real world and found a haven to share. Then the fire began to die into embers and the phone destroyed the illusion. Ginger groaned as she went to answer.

"Ginger, this is Dr. Ellis."

Ginger gasped. "Has something happened to Aunt Dena?"

"Oh, no, dear, I didn't mean to upset you. Dena's fine, just a mite restless and worried, I think. I was wondering if you could call and reassure her. She needs her rest after all the company she's had this afternoon, but something's chewing on her." Dr. Ellis sighed. "Would you know what it might be?"

"I sure do," Ginger admitted, picturing the overbearing Mr. Bennett as she'd last seen him. "Do you think one more short visit would be too hard on her?"

"Not if you can set her mind at rest."

"Then I'll be there in a few minutes."

"We will," Justin corrected as she hung up the phone. "Unless you'd rather see her alone?"

"You don't mind going by the hospital?"

"Heck, no. I like Dena, and I think knowing that we're both working on her project will help her relax. That *is* the problem, isn't it?"

Ginger nodded. "I talked to her for a while this morning, but I guess she's had time since to notice all the questions I couldn't answer."

"Well, we've got more answers for her now." Justin's arm was reassuringly warm around her shoulders as he hugged her close to him. "With a team like us on the project, she can just lie back and heal, right?"

Were they really a team? Ginger found the idea both exciting and disturbing. She didn't want to depend on Justin or have him depend on her. She wasn't ready for emotional demands or the kind of relationship that deepened into a commitment. The whole thing would have scared her to death if she'd had time to think about it. Luckily, she was too busy getting ready to go to the hospital.

Visiting with Dena proved rewarding, as did their stop at the Golden Mill on the way home. Willow Run's attempt at a cocktail lounge turned out to resemble an English pub, but there were plenty of friendly faces to greet them, including Floyd Durosher's.

By the time Justin took her home, Ginger was beginning to believe that the inn project just might work after all. Floyd had come up with a half-dozen enthusiastic suggestions both for his cross-country skiing concession and for developing the lake into a summer attraction.

"Feeling better about the inn's prospects now?" Justin broke into her thoughts as he parked in front of Dena's house.

"Much, thank you. It's nice to know that other people want Dena to succeed as much as we do."

"I'm just sorry to see this day end." Justin shut off the motor and helped her out of the car. He pulled her close against his side as they climbed the slippery porch steps. "I'd sort of pictured us spending a long evening alone in front of that fire, eating popcorn and—"

"Fending off the dog?" Ginger couldn't resist asking as she heard Mischief's bark of greeting. She was afraid to confess that she'd had the same delightful plan in mind. "I'd ask you in, but we both have a lot to do tomorrow and..."

"And it's getting late," Justin finished for her, claiming her lips with a kiss that made her want to forget there was a tomorrow. She swallowed a groan as he stepped away from her. "In deference to your neighbors, I'll be on my way before the beast gets any louder. I'll call you as soon as I set up an appointment at the bank."

"I'll be waiting." Ginger watched him walk away, knowing that her eagerness for his call had little to do with financing the inn. She just wanted to be with him, a disturbing realization that continued to haunt her long after she was settled in bed with Mischief snuggled up beside her.

Just what was he letting himself in for? Justin asked himself the next morning as he finished a forty-five-minute discussion with Clyde Hutchinson, the head of the Willow Run First National Bank. Instead of working on the papers Cynthia had left on his desk, he'd spent most of the morning convincing Clyde to meet with Ginger to discuss the inn project.

Talk about looking for trouble. He combed his fingers through his already tousled hair and leaned back in his chair. Sleep had been pretty elusive last night, but the

dreams that had come near dawn had been even more potent than his memories of kissing Ginger. He hadn't been
this miserable since adolescence. And here he was setting
himself up to spend the afternoon with the cause of his discomfort. A glutton for punishment, that's what he was.

He grinned. But what a challenge! He ached to see those
sexy hazel eyes glow with desire, to touch her and kiss her
until her hunger matched his own. Once that happened . . .
What? His mental replay of last night's sensuous dream
crashed in flames. Make love, then watch her drive away?
Send her back to California with his best wishes and a
promise to call from time to time? If each kiss left him
craving more, making love to her would bond him to her
forever.

He welcomed the interruption of a ringing phone. Work
was manageable—emotional entanglements were a foreign
territory he wasn't sure he was ready to explore. Maybe he
should back off once they had their meeting with Clyde.
Ginger was an experienced businesswoman; she really didn't
need him holding her hand once they got the ball rolling.
But he wanted to hold a lot more than her hand—which was
probably the best reason of all for him to cool things before
it was too late.

Ginger's head was spinning as she drove away from the
bank. Though it was only four-thirty, she was exhausted,
but she couldn't go home yet. Dena would never rest until
she had a report of everything that had happened.

If only she wasn't so confused over what she could only
label as Justin's overnight change of heart. Which she
should be grateful for, she told herself firmly. One of them
had to have the good sense to pull back from the attraction
blazing between them, and she'd certainly failed to last
night. If he could cool it, more power to him. Romance

would only complicate her life. Right now she needed a friend, not a lover.

Her heart ached as she ignored the might-have-beens and focused her energy on the real problems she still had to conquer. She turned a deaf ear to the tiny voice that whispered it was already too late to pretend noninvolvement. Dena would be thrilled with the bank's agreement to back the project. That was all that was important—wasn't it?

As she set the renovations in motion during the week, Ginger could almost believe that the answer to that question was *yes*. Only at night, when she dropped into bed too exhausted to even read, did the longings return to haunt her. In her dreams the pleasant, helpful and always charming Justin, who consulted with her daily, turned back into the romantic, sexy man who'd started a crazy earthquake inside her even before their first kiss.

Why had he changed? What had happened after their kiss good-night on her doorstep? Sometimes when she caught him watching her, she thought the hunger was still blazing in those sexy gray eyes. But when she moved toward him, it seemed to disappear, replaced by the warmth of friendship. And, blast it, that wasn't what she wanted at all.

Even Sandy commented on the change as they shared lunch Friday noon, the day before Dena was to be released from the hospital. "What's with you and Justin, Ginger? I haven't seen him over here since Sunday. Did you two have a fight?"

"Oh, no, we've both just been busy. He does have a business to run, and I've been buried with details since I got the crews started on the inn. Plus he has been helping me with the financial arrangements, and that's taken a lot of his time." The words sounded fine, but she couldn't meet her friend's gaze.

"I don't remember the factory being open evenings, and the crews go home nights." Sandy's tone was light, but when

Ginger stole a peek at her, she could see real concern in her friend's face. "I really thought you two had something special going, Ginger. You didn't brush him off the way you used to, did you?"

"What do you mean?" The question surprised her so much she forgot to be cautious about letting her feelings show. "Justin and I were always just friends."

"Maybe that's the way you felt then, but he had a crush on you before he graduated and left Willow Run."

"Oh, come on, that was in high school, Sandy. Everybody has crushes then, it doesn't mean you don't outgrow them. Look how crazy you were about Barry what's-his-name."

"I was fifteen and I forgot him the moment I started dating Robert."

"Well, I'm sure Justin forgot me the moment he discovered college girls." Ginger swallowed hard. Why did her comments about the other women Justin might have known make her feel so hollow? She didn't want Justin to care about her, did she? The ache inside her made it clear that she did, most emphatically.

"What happened, Ginger? I don't mean to pry, but you don't look any happier than Justin these days."

For a moment she clung to her facade, then she let it go with a sigh. "I wish I knew, Sandy. Sunday night I really thought we were getting close, then Monday Justin was all business. And, well, I think maybe it's better that way."

"Better? When you're this miserable? Give me a break." Sandy's unladylike snort made Ginger smile.

"Maybe it hurts now, but don't you think it would be a lot worse to get involved, and then leave? I'm only here to help Dena, you know. I have a business and a life waiting in Seaview. I don't really belong in Willow Run, and Justin does."

"Did you tell him that?" Sandy's frown deepened.

"He's known it from the beginning. I think maybe that's why he's pulled back. He doesn't want to be hurt and neither do I."

"Maybe you could work something out." Sandy didn't sound too confident.

"Love conquers all only in romantic movies, Sandy. Real life is much more complicated." Ginger gave the words extra emphasis, but they didn't make her feel one bit better. Why in the world had she brought love into this? What she felt for Justin was just a potent physical attraction complicated by an old friendship. Love happened to other people; she was too smart to get involved with feelings that couldn't be controlled.

Sandy shook her head. "I think you're out of your mind. You aren't even giving yourself a chance to fall in love."

Ginger forced a chuckle. "I tried that once and decided the emotion was vastly overrated. I like my life just the way it is—or was. Rewarding, but uncomplicated."

"Don't you ever want a husband and family?" The shock in Sandy's face added to Ginger's empty feeling.

"Some of us aren't suited for domesticity, Sandy. Look at my mom, she was miserable trapped here with me. She's in her element running the resort in Florida."

"You aren't your mother."

"I'm not going to make the mistakes she did, that's for sure. I'm a woman of the nineties. I don't have to settle for anything less than what I want out of life."

Sandy sighed. "I guess you know yourself better than anyone, but, Ginger, don't set your sights too low. You've always had the drive to succeed. You could have it all—including love—if you'd give yourself a chance."

Ginger had changed the subject then, but she found her thoughts returning to the conversation often during the next week, as she did her best to help Dena adjust to her altered life now that she was out of the hospital. The transition wasn't easy for either of them.

Dena woke each day brimming with ideas and the desire to put them into motion. She had little patience with the exercises she was supposed to do and depleted her energy arguing with Ginger and the nurse who came by twice a day to help with her physical therapy. Ginger tried to keep pace with Dena's changing plans, but it was a losing battle. Still, it did keep her from thinking about Justin—most of the time.

She'd almost convinced herself that she was getting over the attraction when the phone rang late Thursday afternoon. Since it was the twentieth call of the day, she snatched up the receiver and growled a less-than-friendly "hello."

"Things going badly, Ginger?" Justin sounded disgustingly cheerful.

Happiness flooded through her like sunshine. "Hi, Justin. Sorry for my bear imitation, but the phone's been ringing off the hook most of the day and Dena's just settled down for a nap. She has her bridge group here this evening, so she's resting up."

"Do you play with them?"

"Heavens, no. I'm no match for that bunch of card sharks. Why, what's up?" For some stupid reason her heart was pounding so hard she wondered if he could hear it.

"Well, I've been working on something for the past couple of days and I'd kind of like to show it to you, if you're free for dinner tonight." Justin's voice held a mixture of caution and excitement in spite of the casualness of his invitation.

"Oh, I think Dena can spare me, since she'll have seven of her cronies to wait on her."

"Hum, do I detect a touch of cabin fever?"

"A full-blown case," Ginger admitted, feeling better than she had in a week. "Between overseeing all the renovations and trying to keep Dena from overdoing, I am slowly losing my mind."

"Then plan to escape about six, okay? We'll have a quiet dinner and talk."

"Sounds good to me." Like heaven.

"I've missed you, Ginger." His voice caressed her ear, then she heard a crash and curse in the background. "Gotta go. See you later." The receiver banged down, breaking the connection before she could say a word.

"I've missed you, too, Justin. I just didn't realize how much until now." Because of her fear of involvement, she'd never dare admit that to him, of course, but Mischief seemed pleased to hear her confession.

"Was that something about the inn?" Dena's voice echoed from the bedroom. "Has something else gone wrong?"

Ginger swallowed a sigh of frustration. How could Dena get well if she never followed Dr. Ellis's orders about resting every afternoon. She hurried down to her aunt's room. "It was Justin calling to ask me out for the evening. Seems he thought I might be corrupted by listening to you and your buddies gossiping."

"Fat chance, he just wants to spend some time with you." Dena's grin widened. "Anyway, I'm glad he's getting you out of here. You deserve some fun, Ginger. You've done nothing but work since I got out of the hospital. Sometimes I feel so guilty about putting everything off on you. If I could just—"

"If you'd just relax, you'd get your strength back a lot faster." Ginger broke into the familiar refrain. "And for your information, I am having fun. I've loved every minute of working on the inn. It's like creating my own fantasy world, only I have help from you and half the people in Willow Run."

"It has been good for the town, hasn't it? I know how much Robert and some of the other local businessmen have appreciated your orders for materials and contracts for work."

Ginger grinned. "Since I blackmailed Clyde Hutchinson with Mr. Bennett's statement that he'd bring in a totally outside crew, I really wanted to make it a community effort. Besides, there are a lot of talented workers in this town and the inn needs all the help it can get."

"That bad?"

"There've been a lot of years of neglect, Dena. We're going to have to replace more pipe and wiring than we thought, and some of the gorgeous hardwood floors are rotted in spots. We may only be able to open on a limited basis for this summer, but everyone has promised that the place will be fully ready by next year's ski season."

"So will I." Dena's determination underlined the words. "Even if I have to do those accursed exercises twenty times a day. I'm going to be walking on my own before we open this summer and fully recovered by fall. You can count on it."

"Never doubted it for a moment," Ginger assured her. "Now get some rest or you'll never make it through that marathon gossip session you call a bridge game."

"We call it news exchange." Dena shifted carefully on the bed, then yawned. "And I'm already several weeks behind."

Ginger closed the door, then ran upstairs. What in the heck was she going to wear tonight and what could Justin want to show her?

"The Hungry Miner okay?" Justin asked as he started the car. "It's not the Candlelight, but the food's good. This is Italian night and their lasagna—"

"Say no more, I'm sold." Ginger smoothed down her green-and-black ski sweater, glad she'd opted for her matching wool slacks and black boots. "Now what did you want to show me?"

"Nothing yet, that's dessert. Right now we're just going out to dinner so you don't turn into a total grouch." Justin's grin took any sting from his words. "Besides, I like being with you, and we've hardly had a chance to talk since Dena got out of the hospital."

"You should come by the inn more often—that's where I am most days. Well, half the time, anyway. I keep running back to the house to show things to Dena, then it's back to the inn to make sure things are going along and... Well, you get the picture."

"Dena must be dying of frustration since she can't supervise herself."

Ginger sighed. "It's really hard on her. She cares so deeply about the place, she can't help being miserable. She should be the one inspecting everything and making all the decisions. It's her dream."

"That's not what I heard." Justin pulled into the parking lot beside the battered old café.

Ginger caught the teasing inflection in his tone. "What do you mean?"

"I had coffee with a couple of the guys yesterday and they said you were calling the shots and doing a terrific job of it." His eyes met hers and she felt as though someone had turned up the heater in the car.

"You could come out and see for yourself."

"Is that an invitation for a personally guided tour?" There was a challenge in his gaze that accelerated her heartbeat.

Ginger couldn't resist the dare. "Any time, you know that." She tried to concentrate on meeting his gaze, but his softening lips distracted her. How she longed to sample them again, to lose herself in the magic that he . . .

She reined in her imagination, realizing where it was leading her. Business dinner, Ginger, she told herself firmly. Nothing has changed since you talked to Sandy, so keep it light. "Dena would probably enjoy a report from you, too, since you were the one with whom she first shared her vision."

"I may be over to talk to her tomorrow. Meantime, I smell lasagna, don't you?" Justin was out of the car before she could reply.

Could he be as uncertain about this date as she was? Ginger wondered as he hurried her into the deliciously scented warmth of the café.

Justin took a deep breath of the spicy air, wishing that he was hungry for food instead of Ginger. When he'd made this date, he'd been sure that he was over his adolescent crush, but one look from those mesmerizing green-flecked, golden-brown eyes and he'd slipped right back into emotional quicksand. Keeping his distance obviously wasn't any more effective now than it had been in high school.

So what was the alternative? he asked himself as he guided Ginger toward the corner booth. Give in to his desire? Forget that she had another life and pursue her as he would have any other woman that attracted him so strongly? Well, why not? She had the ability to make him miserable long distance, so up close and really personal had to be an improvement.

"What are you grinning about?" Ginger found the slightly wicked slant of his lips fascinating.

"You. Me. Being here together." Justin leaned across the narrow table, conscious of their knees touching beneath it and aching to hold her in his arms. "I want to spend more time with you, Ginger. We started something two weeks ago and I want to explore it further. What do you say?"

Ginger gasped, shocked by Justin's straightforward declaration, though she realized at once that she shouldn't be surprised. The Justin she remembered had always been honest. He took her hand, caressing her fingers as he lifted them to his lips.

"I know you feel it, too, Ginger. There's been something simmering between us since that first afternoon. I've tried to ignore it, but I can't. And I really don't want to. Won't you give us a chance to find out where it leads?"

His lips seared the flesh of her palm and the light tickling of his tongue sent shivers down her spine as the look in his smoky eyes ignited the flames within her. Her throat was dry, her lips arid as she tried to draw in a breath. "I—I can't ignore it, either," she whispered, "but I'm afraid."

He nibbled at her fingertips. "Me, too, but that's not going to stop me this time."

This time? Ginger frowned. Had Sandy been right after all? Before she could ask for an explanation, the waitress arrived and Justin turned his attention to joking with her as he ordered wine and enough food to satisfy a small army.

By the time the woman left, Justin seemed content to change the subject and Ginger slowly relaxed as they discussed the renovations and the inn's future prospects. Still, she could feel the building tension beneath the easy conversation. It reminded her of the electricity that crackled in the still, hot air before a summer thunderstorm and the same restless excitement filled her.

Oddly enough, the tension seemed to add zest to her appetite as they attacked the lasagna. Stuffed with rich food and a bit dizzy from the even spicier sensations whenever their eyes met, she accepted an after-dinner glass of wine. She lifted it to toast him. "To explorations."

"And discoveries," Justin replied, his gaze heavy with sensual promise.

· Nervous now that the meal was over, Ginger set her glass down after a sip and sought a safer topic. "When you called, didn't you say you had something to show me?"

Justin chuckled. "I sure did. Can't imagine how I got distracted from my original reason for this meeting." His gaze moved over her face like a caress and she felt the warmth of it burning in her cheeks as he took several folded sheets of paper from his coat pocket, opened them up and passed them across the table to her. "What do you think of these?"

Ginger spent several minutes staring at the neatly drawn pictures that were spread across the pages. Beautiful rustic antique couches, chairs, tables, even a few beds and chests adorned the sheets. "What is this?" she asked at last.

"Doesn't that look like the kind of furniture you're going to need for the inn?" Justin continued to smile at her smugly.

"No, it looks like the kind of furniture we wish we could have for the inn. I've spent some time in the attic and there are maybe two dozen pieces that can be repaired and put into use, but the rest is either junk or too fragile for a hotel. We're going to have to do a lot of shopping around to find enough furniture that we can afford. Why?"

"What would you say if I told you that the furniture in those drawings will be available at competitive prices?"

"That we couldn't compete in the antiques market. Besides, anything this good would be too valuable to put out for public use. I've been to ski resorts, Justin—the guests aren't very careful." Ginger sighed, her eyes drawn to the handsome lines of a chest. "I'd like some of these pieces for myself, though."

"Thank you." His grin broadened.

"What are you..." Ginger let it trail off, suddenly realizing what the pictures represented. "Are these your designs, Justin?"

"Guilty."

"You actually manufacture this kind of furniture?"

"We've done a few special orders in antique styles, but never a whole line. In fact, it wasn't until I started thinking about what would be right for the inn that I even considered it. That's when I realized that there should be a good market for furniture that has the style and detail of handwork, but is built to take the abuse of modern use."

Ginger fought her rising excitement as she pictured the pieces scattered about the mammoth main room and filling the guest rooms as they were finished. "This would be perfect, but there is no way we could afford it, Justin. You know our budget. We've already had to go over it for plumbing and wiring, thanks to some nasty little surprises the crews have uncovered."

"You haven't heard the prices yet."

"You've already worked them out?"

"I've even made appointments with several of my best customers in Denver. This furniture won't be quite as reasonable as our modern stuff, but I doubt they'll be much above the prices of hotel-quality furniture. And I can offer Dena better terms than she'd get anywhere else. In fact, I might even give her a rate in return for advertising in the brochures she'll be sending out. A good showcase is worth it."

Ginger traced the lines of a graceful table. "I just can't believe you could produce these in numbers... They look like...well, like antiques."

"So I'm a genius. That's the fun of having my own factory. I can do things like this. Wait till you see pictures of the special Victorian furniture I did for a client in Phoenix. She has an art gallery and she wanted the look without spending a fortune. She was so happy with the pieces, she ordered a few for her home, too." He took her hands. "Being creative is the best part of my work. It beats shuffling papers and hustling for orders.''

"You really love it, don't you?'' She could read the emotion in his face, but a part of her demanded confirmation.

Justin nodded. "When I left Willow Run, I thought anything would be better than being trapped in the family business. But when I had to take over… Well, I decided that since I couldn't change the circumstances, I'd change the business. It took a while, but now we're set up to do a variety of styles and real quality furnishings. We all enjoy it more.''

"That's terrific. Loving what you do makes the work worthwhile.'' She forced a smile to go with the words, though a part of her heart broke at this proof of how deeply he was tied to Willow Run. If she'd had any illusions about his leaving when Michael could take over the factory, she could forget them now.

"Why don't I come out to the inn tomorrow afternoon, so you can give me that tour you promised? We can work out approximately how many pieces you'll need for your summer opening, then we can take the drawings and the rough figures over and show them to Dena. What do you think?''

"Sounds good to me. I know Dena will be thrilled to see them. She's been fussing about furniture ever since I gave her a complete inventory of everything in the attic.''

Justin picked up the pages, folded them and put them back in his pocket, then took her hands. "That's enough about business. Now we need to plan the rest of our evening. Where would you like to go and what would you like to do?''

Her heart skipped a beat as their eyes met, then began to quicken as her mind presented a number of highly exciting possibilities. "What are my choices?''

"We could go to the Candlelight and dance to the juke-box or catch the late movie and neck in the balcony. Or how about a drive out to the ridge to admire the scenic view of distant Crestline? It's terrific now that Snow Shadow is in operation. They have lights on half the mountain. Looks real pretty by moonlight."

"Sounds like you've already seen the view." She meant the words to be teasing, but found it hard to ignore the twinges of jealousy.

"I think having you beside me would improve the view significantly." He spoke softly, his fingers tightening over hers. "And it would give us a chance to be alone for a while, something that is impossible at my house and at Dena's."

"So let's go see that view." Ginger pushed aside the last of her doubts about the future and smiled up at him. There was no use dwelling on what could never be. They had now—tonight, however long she was here—that would have to be enough. She'd denied her feelings too long already. It was time for explorations and discoveries.

Chapter Seven

The drive to the ridge turnoff seemed to take no time at all as the highway was nearly empty of traffic this late in the evening. Justin slowed once they left the pavement, for the narrow gravel road was still snow packed.

"Guess this area doesn't get as much use now as it did when we were teenagers," Ginger observed.

"Don't tell me a proper young lady like you spent much time out here," Justin teased.

"Actually, I didn't. I just heard rumors."

Justin laughed. "Things have changed since those days. See?" He waved a hand at the open area ahead. Though it was ridged with tire tracks, there wasn't a single car parked there.

"Looks kind of empty, doesn't it?" A shiver of anticipation traced down Ginger's spine.

"I don't mind." Justin parked on the crest of the ridge. "Do you?"

"Not a bit." Ginger gasped as she caught her first glimpse of the fairyland of lights that seemed to dance between the dark shadows of forest on the flanks of the mountain across the narrow valley that separated them from Crestline. The new ski development rose above the small town, and she could see the dim silhouettes of the lodge and outbuildings against the pale snow. "This is incredible."

"Worth the drive?" He shut off the motor and slid over to put his arm around her shoulders.

"Definitely. I just can't imagine why there aren't more people here to see this view."

"As I recall, those who used to come out here weren't exactly interested in the view." Justin's chuckle seemed to set off a tremor inside her.

Ginger turned to face him, shivers of excitement racing over her cooling skin, her heart pounding wildly. "Maybe they stay away because it's too cold this time of year," she suggested, suddenly conscious of the intensity of his gaze. She had to look away to hide her chaotic emotions; being this vulnerable to a man was a new and somewhat frightening experience.

"Don't you think I can keep you warm?" Justin caressed her chin as he tilted her face back up, then seeing the anxiety in her eyes, he gently kissed the tip of her nose. "Don't be afraid, Ginger, and please, don't hide your feelings from me. This is all as new to me as it is to you."

"Oh, Justin." The trembling inside her increased as his lips claimed hers and she surrendered to the seductive magic of losing herself in sensation. She discovered that she loved touching Justin's slightly beard-roughened cheek and burying her fingers in the springy curls on the back of his neck. She cuddled closer. How had she lived so long without knowing this wondrous ache of longing, this strange feeling of not being quite complete without Justin's arms around her?

Justin felt the change in Ginger the moment her lips parted beneath his. She moved closer to him and the barriers he'd sensed each time he'd touched her before seemed to have melted away. Desire coursed through him like molten lava, testing the strength of his willpower.

The kiss seared Ginger, leaving her dizzy and weak when Justin finally broke the mind-blowing contact, pulling away slightly as he drew in a deep breath. It took all her fading self-control to keep from pulling him back against her.

"So much for taking it slow and easy," Justin murmured as the pounding ache of desire announced the depth of his need for her. He had to get control of himself now or risk frightening her into hiding behind her independence once again.

"We seem to have progressed from simmering to boiling rather quickly," Ginger agreed as sanity reluctantly asserted itself. "Too quickly."

"Right." Justin turned to stare out at the view, not seeing it, but not trusting himself to touch her again. "But how do we get back to simmer, Ginger? Keeping my distance sure didn't help." And, damn it, he didn't want to go back. He'd tasted the passion in her kiss. She might deny it, but she was as eager for his touch as he was to caress her.

A dozen reasons why they should retreat filled her mind, but they just melted away when she looked at his shadowed profile. Instead of answering, she reached out to trace the hard line of his lips and felt them tremble beneath her fingertips. "I know we can't go back, Justin, but I think we should be careful about going on with this. We're not the kind of people who can handle casual affairs. What we feel now could end up hurting us both."

Ginger's words did little to cool the burning within him, but he knew she was right. Sighing, he caught her hand and held it tight against his chest so she could feel the pounding of his heart. "I'm willing to sit here all night looking at the view and talking about furniture if that's what you want, but I'd really prefer kissing you a few more times before we head back to Willow Run.''

Though his tone was light, Ginger sensed the seriousness behind his statement. He was letting her know that she could set the pace, that he would respect her decision. She loved him for his consideration and hated him for forcing her to decide. Deep down, she realized that she simply wanted him to kiss her until she was too lost in passion to deny him anything.

''Maybe a few more kisses wouldn't hurt,'' she murmured, ignoring the warning voice in her mind. ''But next time I think we'd better bring Mischief along to chaperon.''

''Next time.'' Justin drew her close again, tasting her lips lightly, then moving on to memorize her face with his kisses. Her words gave him hope. All he needed was a chance to convince her that they belonged together.

Friday was a golden day, warm for early February, full of sunlight and the promise of spring. Ginger smiled as she made her second trip of the day to the inn—this time, she was meeting Justin there. Her pulse rate bounced at the prospect of being near him and she felt like singing in spite of the restless night she'd spent. Maybe she'd been wrong to be afraid of getting close. Maybe there was a way.

She pushed such speculation from her mind as she pulled into the debris-strewn parking lot and looked up at the huge old building. Two men were carrying building materials into the inn, while three others moved cautiously along the outside of the second floor, repairing and repainting the window frames and sills. The rhythm of hammers underscored the sounds of talk and laughter from within.

Having already spotted Justin's car, Ginger hurried across the muddy lot and climbed the stairs to the open door, then skidded to a stop. Justin was there all right, but he wasn't alone. A sexy blonde stood at his side, smiling up at him with the hungry look of a dieter at a bakery counter.

"Ginger, hi, it's about time you got here. I thought I might have to start exploring on my own." Justin's grin reached out to her like a friendly hand and for a moment everyone else ceased to exist, then the blonde moved between them.

"Is that everything you need, Justin?" she asked, fluttering her eyelashes at him.

"That'll do it, Cynthia. Thank you for bringing the papers out to me." Justin slipped an arm around Ginger before he introduced her to his secretary, explaining, "I forgot my cost projections for the new line and Cynthia brought them out to me. Saves us stopping by the factory on our way to Dena's."

"I wouldn't mind a tour of your factory," Ginger told him. Just his secretary? She watched the blonde's eyes as she gushed about the new designs and knew at once that Cynthia was hoping for more. That didn't surprise her, but the knife thrust of jealousy that stabbed through her when she thought of them working together came as a shock.

"Hi, Ginger, Justin. Looks like the gang's all here." Sandy's bright greeting interrupted her dark thoughts and Ginger was glad to escape Cynthia's baleful glances.

"What are you doing out here?" Ginger asked after she'd hugged both Sandy and Joey. "I thought you told me Doc wanted you to stay home and take it easy these days?"

"Not on a day like today." Sandy giggled. "I'm going crazy staring at four walls and I'm dying to see what you've done with this place. Besides, Joey wanted to see where Daddy's been working." She looked around. "Where is Robert, anyway?"

"I don't know, I just got here," Ginger admitted. "When I left this morning, he was upstairs measuring the bedrooms so he could give me an estimate on the cost of wall-papering about half of them.''

"Want to see Daddy," Joey announced. "Where's Daddy?"

"Hey, sport, how about you and me going looking while your mama talks to Ginger?" Justin winked at Ginger as he scooped up the giggling boy.

"You're an angel, Justin," Sandy said, then she turned to Ginger. "Joey's getting to be more than I can handle these days. It's not that he's being bad, he's just so active I can't keep up with him and thanks to you, Robert's so busy..." She stopped. "And I do mean thanks, Ginger. The extra money from working on the inn is really going to make a difference to us.''

"Robert's doing a fabulous job, Sandy. Thanks to him, the store is giving us a discount on all the materials and Robert is supervising the crews doing the painting and pre-paring the walls for papering. I'm just sorry we're keeping him away from home and you.''

"Don't pay any attention to my griping, Ginger. He wouldn't be home, anyway. He's been at the store every day since Daddy had his heart attack. The place would have closed if it hadn't been for Robert, and we would have had to leave Willow Run if Daddy hadn't offered Robert a part-nership.'' Sandy sighed, then her smile brightened. "But that's ancient history. I want my tour of the inn.''

"Are you sure?" Ginger surveyed the chaos skeptically. "The place is a safety hazard with all the work going on.''

"I'll be careful. Shall we start here? Tell me exactly what you're planning to do with this room.''

Within moments, Ginger's enthusiasm overruled her doubts about showing Sandy around the building. Sharing her vision of the inn with Sandy seemed to validate her dreams. She could actually see the way the big room would look, picture it filled with happy tourists enjoying the—

A sharp cracking sound from above cut through Ginger's thoughts and she looked up just as someone shouted a warning. For a moment it was like a scene from a movie. The support beam above them seemed to wiggle, to shake, then with a horrendous splintering sound one end split from the wall. As the threat finally penetrated her stunned mind, Ginger grabbed Sandy and shoved her away, then dived after her.

The crash was deafening and the floor seemed to rock beneath her. Dust, splinters and all manner of other debris rose in a cloud, choking Ginger as she tried to scream. More rained down on her as a moment of shocked silence followed the violent explosion of sound. Then the shouts began.

Ginger sat up slowly, shaking her head and coughing to get rid of the particles that coated her skin and clothing and filled her mouth. Her arms and legs seemed to be working all right, though she felt a whole new crop of bruises hatching as she got to her knees and looked around. "Sandy, Sandy, are you okay?"

A low moan was the only answer. Ginger's throat closed with terror as she stared at the huge beam, seeking Sandy. A chair, several sawhorses and other building materials protruded from under the beam, but there was no sign of Sandy.

"Ginger." The word was more whimper than call, but Ginger followed the sound and became nearly giddy with relief as she located Sandy lying safely under a worktable.

"Sandy, are you okay?" Ginger scrambled to Sandy's side just as her friend began to move. "Did I hurt you when I pushed you down?"

"What happened?" Sandy tried to sit up, then sank back with a groan, holding her huge abdomen. "Oh, the beam fell."

"Sandy? Where are you?" Robert's voice, frantic with fear, boomed above all the others.

"Over here," Ginger shouted, fear shivering through her as she watched Sandy's face grow pale as perspiration broke out on her forehead. "Is it the baby, Sandy?" she gasped, sickness burning in her throat. "If this hurt the baby..."

Robert dropped to the floor beside Ginger, his big hands moving carefully as he eased Sandy out from under the table. Her whimper of pain stopped him. He turned to Ginger, his face nearly as pale as Sandy's. "Did it hit her?"

"No, I saw it coming and pushed her out of the way. It must have been the fall. I couldn't help..."

"She saved us both," Sandy murmured. "I'm okay, I think, but my back hurts and I think the baby is coming. If you could carry me to the car..." She tried to move, then settled back with a groan.

Robert looked helpless for a moment, then seemed to get hold of himself. "Get that new door, will you, Jack," he ordered. "We can put her on that to take her to the hospital."

"Where's Joey?" Sandy's voice sounded a little stronger now that she was holding Robert's hand.

"I left him in the kitchen with Tim. He'll be safe enough there for the moment."

"I'll go get him," Ginger offered, recognizing the rising panic in Sandy's face.

Strong hands lifted Ginger to her feet and for a moment she nestled in the haven of Justin's arms. Then he stepped away to help Robert and Jack as they gently lifted Sandy and eased the wooden door under her to protect her back.

"I brought the van today," Jack said. "There's plenty of room in it for the door. Let me back it up to the porch, then we can load her in and I'll drive you into town."

The matter-of-fact planning helped Ginger regain her own sense of control. "Was anyone hurt?" she asked. "Anyone

else need to go to the hospital?'' She scanned the faces of the
men that were now gathering around. "Somebody take a
count, make sure that everybody is accounted for. And then,
I'll—" A wail and the sound of running feet stopped her
midsentence.

"Joey!" Sandy's gasp was echoed by Robert. "Oh, dear,
he can't see me like this, he'll be terrified."

Justin moved immediately, scooping Joey up before the
little boy could reach the knot of adults. He quickly headed
the other way, asking Joey if he'd heard the big bang. Ginger followed them on knees that seemed to wobble.

Joey's answers showed little interest in the fallen beam.
"Where's Mommy?" he asked, sniffling. "I'm scared." The
words tore at Ginger's heart, yet she understood Sandy's
feelings. Joey was far too young to understand why his
mother had to lie still on the door when he needed to be in
her arms. She sought desperately through her mind for
something to distract him.

"Do you like kittens, Joey?" she asked as they reached
the relative quiet of what would eventually be the inn's office.

"Kitties?" Teary blue eyes turned in her direction.

Ginger forced what she hoped was a reassuring smile. She
had no experience with children and Joey needed comfort
so badly. "Last week I found a mama cat and four babies
in one of the outbuildings. The mama was pretty wild at
first, but now everyone has been feeding her and she lets us
pet her babies. Would you like to see them?"

Joey nodded, his attention fully caught. "Can I have
one?"

"Well, they're too little to leave their mama now, but I'd
be happy to take you out to see them." Ginger glanced at
Justin, but he seemed almost unaware of her as he set Joey
down.

"Why don't you two go see the kittens," he said. "I'll tell Sandy that Joey is okay and see if I can lend a hand with the door."

"Okay, fine." Ginger swallowed hard, not sure she wanted to be left alone with a three-year-old. "We'll be in the old carriage house." She took Joey's hand and led him out the side door and across the muddy ground to the smaller structure.

The next half hour was the longest Ginger had ever lived through. Worry about Sandy distracted her so much she had trouble following Joey's constant chatter. Even while they played with the kittens under the watchful gaze of the long-haired black mother cat, Ginger kept one eye on the door, eager for Justin's return. She didn't know what to say to a child or how to make him feel safe. She heaved a sigh of relief when Justin finally arrived.

"Everything go all right?" she asked, only too aware of Joey's sharp little ears.

"They're on their way." Justin's smile didn't quite hide the worry in his eyes as he turned to Joey. "Hey, sport, how'd you like to go to the drive-in for some ice cream?"

"Mommy and Daddy, too?" Joey's quick question told Ginger how little she'd been able to allay his fears.

"Well, no, they had some work to do, so I asked them if Ginger and I could take care of you this afternoon. What do you think of that?" Justin's casual tone didn't fool her for a moment, but she admired his ease with Joey.

"It's okay." Joey's sigh seemed to fill the room. "When will Mommy be back?"

"I don't know, Joey. She asked me to drop you off at your grandma's later. Maybe she thought you'd like to stay overnight with them. What do you think?"

Narrow shoulders rose in a shrug as Joey continued dragging a piece of string for the kittens to chase. Ginger ached to hug Joey, but she felt too awkward. What if he didn't want her hugs?

Justin showed none of her hesitation as he picked Joey up, hugging and tickling him until he giggled. He didn't seem to have any doubts, Ginger noticed. He knew exactly what Joey needed. And he obviously enjoyed giving him reassurance and love. It made her feel warm just watching them together. When Justin had a son of his own . . .

The good feelings vanished in a flash as reality crashed down around her. When Justin had a son, she'd be no-where around to watch him. Some other lucky woman would be the mother of his children, someone who could reach out and give love to a frightened child instead of standing back feeling inadequate. Someone like Dena and not at all like her mother.

Suddenly, watching Justin and Joey hurt too much. "I think I'll go back inside and talk to the crew about what happened." Ginger was eager to escape the carriage house. "You stay with the kittens as long as you like, then we'll go get ice cream."

"You okay?" Justin's gaze probed at her.

"Just worried about what that beam breaking means to the renovations. If everyone working here is going to be in danger, I . . ." She couldn't go on, nor could she admit that the sobs that clogged her throat had nothing to do with the renovation of the old inn.

Justin's frown told her that he'd sensed something was wrong, but he said only, "We'll be in pretty soon."

Ginger stood outside for several minutes waiting for the cold fresh air to blow away her longing for something she could never have, but the ache didn't ease. Finally, she just gritted her teeth and went inside to talk to the men. Work had always been her antidote for pain, so why should this time be any different?

Justin was still shaking his head in confusion as he carried Joey back to the inn a short time later. Was Ginger angry because he'd offered to take care of Joey? That made no sense, yet something had certainly been bothering her when she left the carriage house. Or was she just more concerned about the inn than she was about Sandy? He rejected the idea at once; Ginger loved Sandy, that was obvious. So what could be troubling her?

Much to his relief, Ginger greeted him with a smile. "Jack just got back and he says everything is looking good with Sandy. She's definitely in labor, but her back checked out okay."

"So are you ready to take this young man out for ice cream?"

"I'll even spring for a hamburger. What do you say, Joey?" Ginger grinned at Joey, trying hard to match Justin's easy tone. She'd never be comfortable with children, but she could try faking it for a little while.

Joey's hug when they dropped him off at his grandmother's was positive proof to Ginger that she'd been a success and, much to her surprise, she found it a perfect reward. "He's a great kid," she murmured as they pulled away from the house.

"Don't sound so surprised," Justin teased. "You two seemed to hit it off pretty well."

"That's 'cause you were around. I'm all thumbs when it comes to kids. That's why I never did much baby-sitting when I was growing up."

"You needed a younger brother or sister to practice on. Believe me, you can learn volumes." Justin seemed undisturbed by her confession of inadequacy. "What do you say we head back out to the inn now? You still owe me a tour, you know."

Images of being alone with Justin at the romantic old inn filled her mind, heating her blood. Then memories of the falling beam chilled her. "After what happened, I'm not sure I can face the place again so soon."

"Oh, come on, didn't you tell me that the beam was rotten from that leak in the roof?"

"That's what everyone on the crew said. They were working on that water-damaged section of flooring in the bedroom and all of a sudden it gave way and dropped on the beam. None of them had realized that the water had reached the beam, too, so they hadn't even tested it." Ginger sighed. "Needless to say, the rest of the beams and every other bit of wood in that structure will be tested now."

"Hey, don't be so down. No one was seriously hurt and Mrs. Wallace says Doc expects Sandy to have a normal delivery. It could have been a lot worse." He reached out and pulled her close to his side.

Ginger snuggled against him, gladly resting her head on his shoulder. Just being with him made her feel so special and complete, as though nothing else in the world really mattered. Not that she believed the illusion, she told herself firmly, but it couldn't hurt to enjoy it, could it?

"So do I get my tour?"

"Of course. We have to figure out what furniture we're going to need before we talk to Dena about your designs." She tried to force her mind back to reality, but her heart really wasn't in it.

"Do you still want to talk to her about the furniture today?" Justin sounded surprised.

"When I called Dena from the drive-in, she told me to bring you home to dinner, so why not?" Ginger rested her hand lightly on his thigh, glorying in the way his muscles tensed beneath her fingers. "Are you free?"

"You better believe it." Justin turned his head so he could touch her forehead with his lips. "But is Dena able to cook, or should we pick up something on our way back?"

"Cooking is all she does these days. She claims that it keeps her sane. But she's going to have me fattened up like a Thanksgiving turkey if she doesn't get distracted pretty soon."

Justin's arm tightened. "You feel about right to me."

"You feel pretty good yourself," Ginger murmured, snuggling even closer as Justin turned off the highway and headed up the now well-worn road to the inn.

The area of the inn was deserted now, the building heavily shadowed as the sun dropped toward the mountain peaks. Justin parked near the front door, then turned to kiss her lightly before they got out. "It's going to be a striking building when you get through," he commented. "People will be lining up for rooms once you're ready to open."

"It is quite wonderful, isn't it?" Ginger surrendered to the magic, seeing the inn as it would be by summer, preferring not to remember that she would be back in Seaview long before the inn opened. "Perfect for honeymooners. I think I'll make that a selling point, when I do the advertising. A small resort is much more romantic than a big lodge, don't you think?"

Their eyes met and Ginger felt the compelling power of his desire igniting her own so that the heat blazed through her. She could so easily imagine coming here with Justin, staying in the suite upstairs, making love while the moon smiled through the window at them, then sleeping in his arms.

Swallowing hard, she forced herself to look away. "Shall we go inside? Did you bring something to write on?" She had to stop this fantasizing before it took over her life. She didn't belong here and no amount of daydreaming was going to change that fact. Wanting Justin wasn't enough... was it?

Justin swallowed a curse as he followed Ginger inside. The woman was driving him crazy. One moment he could see the desire burning in her eyes, the next she was babbling about furniture orders. When was she going to give in to her feelings and admit that she wanted him every bit as much as he wanted her?

Tramping through the empty building gave him his answer—it wasn't going to be any time soon. Ginger was all business and, in spite of his frustration, he had to admire her grasp of the details of the project. By the time they returned to his car, he had several pages of notes.

"I hope you're right about Dena cooking plenty," he observed as they headed back down the hill toward Willow Run. "I had an early lunch and I'm starving."

"Me, too." Ginger chuckled. "I've developed an unfortunate appetite since I've been here. I think it's because I'm no longer spending most of my time behind a desk."

"It's the healthy mountain air."

"Right," Ginger agreed, even though she suspected her need to gnaw had more to do with frustration than location. Keeping her hands off him was getting harder with every passing day. Yet how could she give in to her longing to love him, knowing that it would only be temporary, that she would have to kiss him goodbye in a month or so?

The ache that came from even thinking about leaving told her how devastating it would be if she got more deeply involved with Justin. She gladly exchanged the romantic illusions left over from their time at the inn for the friendly chaos of Dena's and Mischief's welcome. Maybe she did need a chaperon to help guard her vulnerable heart.

They'd just finished dessert when the phone rang. "I hope that's Robert calling to say Sandy's had the baby." Ginger bounced to her feet and hurried into the living room to answer.

"Hi, Ginger, how's it going?" The voice was Les Cowan's, not Robert's.

Ginger sank down in the chair, not particularly glad to hear from her partner. "Slowly, Les, but with Dena home from the hospital, we are making progress. It just takes time." She hadn't told him much about the inn during their infrequent calls, so she didn't mention today's setback. "What's up?"

"I got a call today from that Costa Rican client of yours, Enrique Calderon." Les's tone changed, becoming subdued.

Ginger frowned, sensing a problem. "What's on his mind? Wasn't he happy with the annual reports?"

"I don't know. That is, he wouldn't discuss them with me. I explained that you were out of town on family business and offered to take care of anything he needed, but he just said that he'd be in the L.A. area the last week of the month and that he needed to see you then."

Ginger waited a moment, expecting more, but Les didn't break the silence. Finally, she asked, "That's it? He didn't ask any specific questions about his properties?"

"He didn't seem to want to talk to me, Ginger, and I haven't a clue as to why. You did notify him that I was a full partner, didn't you?"

"Of course, I sent the notification out to all our clients, Les." Ginger sighed. "Enrique's special, though. He was my first big client. He really lifted Howard Management from a small business into the big time."

"So what's the story on him? I don't remember you telling me more than just that he was our biggest property holder."

"When I met him, he'd just been burned pretty badly by one of the big management companies. They'd let his properties deteriorate and didn't notify him about some vacancy problems that came about because of their neglect. He came through L.A. on business, stopped by one of his buildings and found out just how bad the situation was."

"And canceled his management contract on the spot?"

"He sued them and won damages. But he couldn't stay around to take care of his buildings himself, so he started looking for a new company. Luckily, one of my clients referred him to me and we hit it off. I just hope that there's nothing wrong with his properties. Did you pull the reports?"

"Checked them all out with Ann. Every one reflects a nice increase over last year. I couldn't find a thing that he should be worried about. Can you come back and meet with him?"

Ginger stared across the room at the fireplace, remembering the romantic Sunday she'd spent here with Justin. "I guess I'll have to, won't I? With Enrique, that's the only way we'll find out what he wants."

She finished the conversation, but didn't hurry back to the dining room. Justin's rumble of laughter reached out to her, but she couldn't respond. Her other life was drawing her back and she felt nothing but dread at the prospect of leaving here. What was happening to her, and how could she recapture her independent spirit before it was too late?

Chapter Eight

The phone rang again, startling Ginger out of her reverie. She picked it up immediately.

"I knew you were waiting for the call, but I didn't think you were that anxious." Robert's voice was full of laughter.

"I just hung up," Ginger explained, relief banishing her other fears. "What's the news?"

"Joey has a little sister, Sarah Lynn, just an ounce short of seven pounds. Mother and daughter are doing just fine. Doc says she's only a week or ten days ahead of schedule, so he doesn't anticipate any problems."

"Thank God," Ginger murmured, closing her eyes for a moment. "If that fall had hurt either of them—"

"Don't even think about it, Ginger. We were all lucky. Now, I have to go. There are a lot of calls to make and I want to be the one to tell Joey. See you tomorrow."

"If you need some time off, the work can wait, Robert. Sandy and Sarah come first." Ginger spoke quickly, aware that she'd be in trouble if the falling beam delayed them very long, but still feeling guilty about what had nearly happened to her best friend.

"Thanks, but I've already talked to Jack and he says replacing that beam won't delay me, so I'll be out there. Take care." He was gone before she could say anything else.

Ginger hurried to the dining room to share the good news, her own phone call easily forgotten as Dena suggested that they open a bottle of wine to toast the new arrival and the furniture order she and Justin had just worked out. Seaview was another world, and everything here was much more exciting—especially when she met Justin's gaze over the rim of her wineglass. The promise in his eyes burned away her doubts and left her aching to be alone with him.

The next week passed in a haze of work and frustration. Though she saw Justin several times, their moments alone were rare and far too short. Then he left Friday to spend a long weekend in Denver meeting with his clients there, showing them the first samples of his new rustic antiques.

He finally called her late Monday evening, sounding weary but happy. "I did it. I've got enough orders for the new stuff to go into full production as soon as we get set up. I may even have to hire a few new people just to keep up with my regular orders."

"I'm really glad you're back. Didn't you hear the weather reports?" She wanted to believe that her irritation came from the worrying she'd done since she'd heard about the approaching cold front, but deep down she knew better. She'd wanted his new line to be a success, but now that it was, it tied him that much more firmly to Willow Run and his factory.

"You didn't think I'd let a little thing like a blizzard keep me away, did you?" His intimate laugh sent shivers down her spine and banished the dark feelings.

"I'm just happy you're home. Now tell me all the details." She let herself slip into his world, sharing his excitement and satisfaction, wishing only that she could be beside him, safe in his arms as he told her about his success.

Thanks to a paralyzing blizzard that struck on Tuesday, closing most roads in the area, work at the inn had to be suspended for two days, putting them further behind schedule. Ginger spent most of her time reassuring Dena, while privately wondering if they'd ever get the inn ready in time to open Memorial Day weekend. Or any other time.

Her mother called twice during the week and, much to Ginger's surprise, the second time she had a solution to the problem Ginger had confided to her. She offered to fly to Willow Run to stay with Dena while Ginger was in California.

Ginger was delighted. "That's super, Mom, but are you sure? Isn't it still tourist season?" She couldn't help being curious about her mother's change of heart. "I wouldn't want you to leave Evan in the lurch."

"Things are going so well he can get along without me for a little while." Her mother chuckled. "Besides, his sisters are coming the last week of February, so they can help out."

"Oh, that is quite a coincidence." Ginger grinned, well aware that her mother had never liked Evan's older sister.

"Isn't it." Her mother's tone positively purred with satisfaction, making Ginger sure that it wasn't a coincidence at all. Not that she'd ever mention it, she decided. She'd just be happy that she could go home knowing Dena was in good hands. Still, it wasn't relief she felt when she hung up the phone; it was depression. Because there was so much to be done before she left, she told herself. Her bad mood couldn't have anything to do with leaving Justin, could it?

Because of the storm delay, she had little time to ponder her feelings and even less time to spend alone with Justin, who seemed to have virtually moved into the factory to supervise the changeover for the new line. Most days, she was so caught up in plans for the inn, Ginger never gave a thought to her impending trip to Seaview. And on the rare occasions when she and Justin stole a few moments alone, she couldn't bear to waste time telling Justin about it. Once she was in his arms, nothing else mattered.

With all the heavy new snow, she and Justin accepted an invitation to spend Saturday following Floyd and Phil through the woods near the inn exploring possible cross-country ski trails. When they returned to the inn late in the afternoon, Justin waved the Duroshers on their way, saying, "We're going to check out a couple of things inside. Thanks for the tour. The trails should be great."

"What are we checking out inside?" Ginger asked, sinking down on the inn's porch with a groan. "All I want now is a long hot bath and about a quart of liniment. I may never walk again."

"Oh, I think I can change your mind." Justin's grin sent her heart into overdrive. "Or at least convince you to postpone that bath for a while." He unlocked the heavy door. "Of course, I'll be happy to help you avoid walking."

Before she could protest, he scooped her up in his arms and carried her inside. "Justin, what are you...?" Her question trailed off as she caught the sweet scent of burning pine and realized that the building wasn't nearly as dark as she'd expected. "What's going on here?"

"If my little brother wants to continue living, there should be a nice fire, candles, a hot dinner and champagne. I thought you could use a little pampering and I'm tired of seeing you only in crowds. How does that sound to you?"

"Like a little touch of heaven." She snuggled closer, slipping an arm around his neck and kissing his still-cold lips. "All we lack is a nice hot tub."

"Oh, what a terrifically decadent idea. That's just what this inn needs. Hot tubs for thawing out skiers." Justin shifted his embrace, slowly releasing her legs, allowing her to slide down along his body even as his arms tightened and he deepened the kiss, taking her breath away.

Heart pounding, Ginger tried to recapture her self-control by focusing on the inn once he freed her lips. "Actually, I'm seriously considering converting the carriage house into a hot tub facility. I talked to Miles and Pete about the feasibility of putting in the plumbing and electricity we'd need, but—"

Justin's lips stopped her words and she lost herself in the sensations that exploded through her. Her body seemed to catch fire, to melt and mold to his. She couldn't think, only feel, as every nerve within her ached for his caress. She slipped her hands under his heavy ski jacket and sweater to find the warmth of him, groaning as his lips ravaged hers.

An eternity of wonder and discovery passed before Justin loosened his embrace and stepped back. "I thought you were tired," he murmured, looking as dazed as she felt.

"I think you just revived me." Ginger looked around, blinking at the changes Michael had made while they were skiing. A small area of floor in front of the fireplace had been swept clean and a mound of blankets awaited them. An ice bucket and champagne glasses caught the firelight and off to one side she could see that a crockpot had been plugged in. "It looks wonderful."

"There's definite hope for the kid," Justin agreed, moving past her to light the candles on the mantel and to switch on the tape player. Soft music filled the air. "Hungry?"

"Starved." She looked up at him, aware that only a part of her craved food. Deep inside, the real hunger waited and only Justin's kisses and caresses could satisfy that need. Could she be in love with him? The answer seemed obvious, yet she feared admitting it, even to herself. To love Justin would be to open herself up to all the pain that came from love. It was far safer to acknowledge only the emptiness in her stomach. "What's for dinner?"

"How does beef stew and French bread sound? And there should be fruit and cheese in the basket with the dishes. Holly promised to put in everything we'd need."

"Sounds like you involved your whole family." Ginger found the idea disturbing. This looked suspiciously like a scene set for a seduction, so how could Justin have asked his brother and sister to prepare it?

"They knew I wouldn't have time to do anything myself today." Justin seemed oblivious to her misgivings as he spread the blankets and cushions on the floor near the crockpot, then knelt down to open the basket. "Isn't this nicer than a restaurant or hurrying home?" He looked up at her, his eagerness for acceptance so obvious that she couldn't resist it.

"Of course it is." She settled herself beside him on the cushions. "I guess I'm just stunned. I had no idea you were planning something like this."

"I like surprising you." He handed her the loaf of bread, then filled two bowls with the fragrant stew. "Besides, I figured this was the only way I was going to spend any time alone with you. Between your helping Dena and my overload of work at the factory, we never see each other."

"Well, this is wonderful and I do appreciate it, but did you tell Dena? If I don't get home before dark—"

He stopped her words with a kiss. "I took care of it. She knows that I planned a special dinner for just the two of us and she approves wholeheartedly, so just relax and enjoy yourself. Forget the rest of the world is even out there."

"With pleasure." Ginger met his gaze as she tasted the stew and for a moment she couldn't even breathe, let alone swallow. Her appetite for anything but his kisses fled and she knew that she could no longer deny her feelings. Love for Justin filled her, spilling over with joy and laughter and a hunger that no amount of food could satisfy.

Stunned by her own emotional response to him, Ginger concentrated on breaking up the chunks of garlic bread to share with Justin. This was going to take some getting used to, she decided as she forced down the food. And what if he didn't feel the same way? What if he meant this just as a fling, a once-in-a-lifetime seduction that... The thought chilled her so much she forced it away. He just had to feel the same way she did.

Justin sensed the change in Ginger even as they talked lazily about the trails they'd explored and Floyd's ideas for the ski shop he wanted to set up in the storeroom off the lobby. What he'd planned as a relaxing, romantic dinner appeared to be making her nervous. She seemed almost afraid to look at him and whenever he tried to steer the conversation from business to more personal topics, she quickly brought it back to the inn.

Was she afraid of being here alone with him? Her passionate response to his kisses when they first came in had been like the answer to all his dreams, but now... He swallowed a sigh. Being patient was getting harder with every passing minute and it didn't seem to be working, anyway. Ginger was falling in love with him, he was almost sure of that. She just needed to admit it to herself, then everything would be fine.

"Ready for champagne?" he asked.

"Oh, yes." Ginger met his gaze and for the first time she didn't even try to hide her feelings. She'd never meant to play games with Justin, so tonight she owed him honesty. She just wished she wasn't quite so afraid of the consequences.

Justin felt the jolt of heat and nearly spilled the sparkling wine. Maybe he wasn't so good at reading her moods after all. She definitely had the look of a woman in love...

His woman, the only one he'd ever really wanted. He offered her a glass.

"How about a toast," Ginger said, her excitement building as their fingers brushed on the slender stem of the glass.

"To us." Justin touched his glass to hers. He wanted to add more, but he didn't. What was happening between them was too fragile, the feelings too new.

"To us." She echoed his words, tasting them with her mind as she did so. Could there be an "us"? Would it really work out somehow? She desperately wanted to believe that they could find a way. She sipped the tickling liquid, already intoxicated by the swirling emotions that just being close to Justin unleashed.

After several aeons of losing himself in the molten depths of her eyes, Justin set their nearly empty glasses aside, then drew her close. He claimed her lips, desperately trying to banish the last of her doubts and questions. This time he demanded an answering passion from her and much to his relief, Ginger responded to his hunger joyously.

Reveling in the wonder of love, Ginger matched his fire with her own. She needed no urging to slip her hands beneath his ski sweater to explore the strong muscles of his back. She happily slipped out of her own sweater and as his kisses moved over her soft skin, she couldn't hold back moans of exquisite pleasure. She ached for more, for a completion she'd never found because she was afraid to surrender control, to trust that love would be enough.

Shaking with his own desire, Justin drew back, feasting his eyes on the pale perfection of her shoulders, the full curve of her breasts, barely concealed now by the wispy lace bra. He traced one finger lightly down the side of her neck and across the pulse beat at the base of her throat. "I'd like to spend every night like this," he whispered. "Maybe that's what we should do, just move out here. What do you think?"

Ginger caught his hand and lifted his fingers to her lips. His words filled her mind with images of delight, adding to her already dizzy longing. It might be only a foolish dream, but she wanted it to be real. "If Dena's well enough to stay alone by the time I get back, maybe we could steal some time here."

The words were out before she thought, but the moment she said them she felt Justin stiffen, and all the wonderful images shattered under a sudden realization—she'd never told Justin about her trip to Los Angeles. She closed her eyes, afraid she'd just destroyed the most perfect moment of her life.

"Get back? From where?"

Ginger swallowed hard, seeking through her mind for the right words, the ones that would banish the tension she heard in Justin's voice. She couldn't look at him, couldn't let him see the guilt that was sweeping over her. Why hadn't she told him? "I...umm...have to fly to L.A. on Monday. My biggest client is coming in from Costa Rica on business and he wants a conference, so..." She let it trail off, sensing that the words were totally inadequate.

Justin stared at her, reading what looked like guilt on her expressive face. Pain slowly replaced the singing desire inside him. What was going on here? He couldn't believe it—she'd planned to leave Monday without a word to him! "When did this come up?" he asked, trying to sound casual as he freed his hand from her suddenly cold fingers.

"Les called a while back to tell me that Enrique wouldn't talk to him. I kept hoping that he'd be able to work something out, but..." Again she ran out of words. How could she make him understand that she'd pretended to herself that she didn't have to go because she didn't want to leave him? She'd never been an indecisive person—at least, not until she'd discovered the magic of being in Justin's loving arms.

"What about Dena?" Justin's gray eyes bored into her, cold and remote. His mouth, once so tender and giving, now looked as though it had been carved in granite. "Who is going to take care of her while you're gone?"

Ginger winced, recognizing she was trapped. "Mom will be with her. She's flying in from Florida Sunday. It's really a lucky coincidence—her sisters-in-law are going to visit the resort, so she's coming here to avoid them."

Her answer to his question came with a pathetic smile that only underlined the guilt in her eyes. Her admission that she'd kept her plans from him was like a knife being driven into his heart. What else hadn't she told him? Did she have someone special waiting for her?

Anger replaced the pain as he realized that to have made all those arrangements she must have known about the trip for at least a couple of weeks. Unable to look at her now, he stared into the dying fire remembering the night Sandy had her baby. Ginger had taken two phone calls after dinner. But he'd been so busy talking to Dena about the new designs that he hadn't wondered about the first one, then he'd forgotten it completely as they celebrated the order and little Sarah's birth.

Ginger sat up, suddenly feeling cold and naked. It was hard to believe that only moments ago she'd blazed beneath Justin's caresses and hungered to feel his body pressed to hers. Shivering, she pulled on her sweater and tried to smooth down her hair. Tears burned in her eyes, but she blinked them back, afraid that once she began crying she'd never be able to stop. All she wanted to do now was escape before her fragile self-control shattered completely.

"Were you planning to tell me, Ginger, or was I just supposed to find out from Dena when I called Monday?" The anger in his voice struck her with the force of a slap.

He hated her now and she couldn't even blame him. Justin's code of honor would brand what she'd done as a form of lying and he'd be right. Her only hope lay in making him understand why she'd hidden the truth, and she wasn't sure she could. Still, the agony inside her made it clear that she had to try.

"Of course I was going to tell you, Justin, but we always had so many more important things to talk about. Besides, I didn't even want to think about going myself. Everything that was happening here seemed so much more... real."

"So it just slipped your mind." He couldn't listen to her excuses and he couldn't bear the pain that shone like unshed tears in her eyes. He began clearing away the debris from their supper—the wonderful, romantic supper he'd planned. If he hadn't been hurting so badly, it would have been funny. When he made a fool of himself, he did a bang-up job of it.

"I meant to tell you tonight, but then we..." Memories of the ecstasy she'd nearly tasted swept over her and she couldn't go on. She grabbed her jacket and headed for the door as the tears spilled down her cheeks. "I'm sorry."

She ran out into the dark night, grateful that they'd come in separate cars, so that she could flee back to Dena's and hide herself away until time to leave for Seaview. She'd been right all along, she told herself bitterly, love had no place in her life. She'd just proved it by destroying every bit of the romance Justin had offered her tonight.

Justin turned at the sound of the door slamming. A part of him ached to go after her, to ask for more explanations. He wanted desperately to believe that it was all a mistake. "One born every minute," he told himself as he shivered in the cooling room, then turned back to his cleaning up.

He'd gotten along without her before; he could do it again. He tried not to think of how close he'd come to making love to her, to making her his own. Then he cursed, unable to deny the fact that he still wanted her. The woman was in his blood like a virulent virus and he hadn't a clue as to what might cure him.

Ginger's headache grew worse the closer she got to Denver. She'd spent a miserable, sleepless night, thanks to her breakup with Justin. Now she had to meet her mother and explain to her why she was going to have to make the long drive back to Willow Run alone. Mom wasn't going to like that, she was sure.

She wished that Dena had been able to ride into the city with her. Dena seemed to have a knack for bridging the gap that had existed between Ginger and her mother for as long as she could remember. But Dena could barely tolerate the short rides to and from the doctor's office.

Ginger sighed. Anyway, she didn't need Dena's company right now since her aunt was angry with her for changing her reservations so she could take a late flight tonight.

At least Mom would have to agree this was more practical than driving into Denver again early tomorrow morning. And maybe by the time she returned, Dena would have forgotten all the questions she'd had about Ginger's dinner date at the inn. Not that Ginger would ever tell anyone about last night's fiasco. She was going to forget it had ever happened. Sure she was, just as soon as it stopped hurting so damned much.

Once she got home it would be all right. In Seaview she'd be so busy getting caught up on everything, she wouldn't even think about Willow Run or Justin or what it felt like to be in love. By the time she had to come back, she'd be over her temporary insanity and ready to concentrate on seeing the inn renovations through to the finish.

She rubbed her aching head as she caught her first glimpse of Denver ahead. If she was so anxious to leave Willow Run, why did she feel so rotten? And why did she keep thinking of all the things she should have said to Justin last night?

She tried to banish him from her thoughts by concentrating on what lay ahead.

Two hours later, she watched as her mother maneuvered the sports car out of the parking area, then smiled and waved to her as she eased her way into the traffic flow. Only when the car vanished did she allow herself to slump against the nearest support.

She felt like a traitor for being so relieved, especially since her mother had been surprisingly enthusiastic about visiting Willow Run and quite understanding about Ginger's not returning with her. The strain had come because Mom wanted to know all about the inn, and everything Ginger mentioned came with wonderful memories of Justin. Why hadn't she realized just how much they'd shared these past weeks, how much a part of her life he'd become?

Stop thinking about him! she instructed herself. Concentrate on what you're going to tell Enrique. Think about the new office that Les says is almost ready to open. Pretend you have a life to go to. That final thought shocked her out of her depression.

What was she thinking? She had a wonderful life in Seaview, a thriving company she'd created. So there wasn't anyone special waiting—that had been her choice. She couldn't allow a few kisses to divert her attention from Howard Management. Justin wanted a wife and a mother for his children; she wanted the satisfaction of building her company to be the biggest and best in the Los Angeles area.

Straightening her shoulders, she headed for the waiting area. Her flight didn't leave for another two hours. That was plenty of time to go through the folder of papers Les had sent her last week—papers she'd barely glanced at when they arrived.

Her concentration didn't improve. Within fifteen minutes, the words on the reports were running together and the only clear image in her mind was Justin's face. She kept seeing the hurt in his eyes instead of the anger that had come later. Cursing herself for a fool, she dug out a pile of change and headed for the bank of pay phones. At least she could call and say a proper goodbye.

When he answered, she had to swallow twice before she could even manage "Hello."

"Ginger?" The happy surprise in his voice brought a fresh burning of tears to her eyes. "Where are you? Dena told me you were leaving tonight instead of tomorrow."

"I'm at the airport in Denver. My flight goes in a while so..." Her throat closed. What was she going to say? For a person who normally planned her business discussions well in advance, she was giving a wonderful imitation of a bubble head. But then, her feelings for Justin had nothing whatsoever to do with business, now did they?

"Oh, I was hoping that your meeting had been called off at the last minute or something." The warmth in his voice faded a little.

"No such luck. Enrique flies into L.A. tomorrow." She took a deep breath. "But I don't want to talk about that. I just wanted...I couldn't leave without at least saying goodbye, Justin. I shouldn't have run out like that last night, but after everything we'd shared..." She couldn't finish the sentence. It took all her self-control not to hang up the phone so he wouldn't hear the sob in her voice.

"That's why I tried to call you tonight. I didn't like having you leave when things were so strained between us. We've been friends for too long and..." He didn't seem to be doing any better at finishing sentences than she was.

Ginger closed her eyes and plunged in. "You had every right to be angry at me last night. I should have told you about the meeting. It certainly wasn't a secret. It's just that whenever we were together, it didn't seem that important. I guess I thought if I ignored it, it would go away."

"Did you want it to go away?" He sounded puzzled.

"Of course not. Enrique's properties are the core of my business. I just didn't want to leave right now. There are so many things still to be done at the inn and Dena's therapy is at a critical stage and..." Why couldn't she just say that she wanted desperately to be with him, that she needed to explore the emotions that had exploded between them last night?

"I don't think you need to worry about the inn—Jack and Robert can keep things rolling there and your mother will help Dena, won't she?" His tone was cooler now, telling her that he'd expected more from her.

"Sure, of course. I'm just being silly. Anyway, I won't be gone that long, I'm sure. I'll probably be back before the weekend." She'd made a mistake, Ginger realized bitterly—there was no way she could tell him what she was feeling over the phone. Calling Justin had just made everything worse, not better. "I'll call you as soon as I get back, okay? We really do need to talk about...about everything."

"Right. And thanks for calling. Have a good flight." He broke the connection before she could say more than goodbye. Feeling even worse, Ginger took two more aspirin and returned to her papers. It promised to be a very long week.

Chapter Nine

Seaview welcomed her with the sunshine and warm temperatures she'd been longing for, but she had little time to appreciate either. Monday passed in a blur, leaving her so exhausted that when she finally returned to her apartment after a business dinner, she didn't even notice the dust or the silence that surrounded her. She simply stripped off her clothes and fell into bed.

Ginger slept like the dead until near dawn when the dream began. She was dancing with Justin, locked in his arms as they swirled around the fully finished main room of the inn. As she lifted her lips to his, he scooped her up and carried her to the second floor, taking her to her favorite room, which was also completely ready.

"What's happening?" she asked, drinking in the heady wine of his scent, touching her lips to his jaw, then moving on to taste the tender skin beneath his ear.

"This is our honeymoon, love, and where else should we begin our life together? Isn't that why you made this room so special, so that it would be ours?'' His hands moved over her body, driving her mad with wanting.

"Yes, yes, oh, yes, Justin.'' She was drowning in sweet sensations, losing herself in the wonder of...

He faded from her arms leaving only emptiness as Ginger woke shivering. "Justin?'' For a moment she reached out, somehow sure that he must be beside her, but she found only the cold sheets. Regret stabbed through her as she sat up.

Ginger looked around, slowly recognizing the elegant beauty of her peach-and-white bedroom. She was home in Seaview, not at the inn. And she was definitely alone. For a heartbeat she was relieved—then something strange happened. Though she'd lived alone contentedly for most of her adult life, this time she felt the emptiness of the silent apartment.

There was no one to talk to or worry about, not even Mischief, who'd nearly driven her mad when she first moved into Dena's house. Here she had no one to need her or want her or even care that she was awake, alone and desperately lonely. The tears she'd refused to give in to before spilled over in a rush she could no longer deny.

"Damn you, Justin,'' she sobbed, "why did you have to make me fall in love with you?''

Hearing herself say the words broke through her sobs. A part of her wanted to deny the truth of her revelation, but she couldn't. She might never admit it to anyone else, but her personal code of ethics demanded that she be honest with herself. After what had nearly happened Saturday night, she couldn't deny the fact that she'd let down her guard and the unbelievable had happened. She'd lost her heart to a man who was absolutely wrong for her.

Feeling as though she no longer controlled her life, she slipped out of bed and padded to the shower. How could she have been so careless? Love demanded too much and hurt too deeply when it ended. She closed her eyes as the spray washed over her.

Tuesday, her day-long conference with Enrique Calderon distracted her from her preoccupation with Justin. She was delighted when Enrique asked her opinion about some new acquisitions that he hoped to turn over to Howard Management. That evening she enjoyed Les's company at dinner, but whenever the conversation lagged, Justin returned to haunt her. Her business coup was somehow less exciting because she couldn't share it with him, and when Les brushed a casual good-night kiss across her lips, she felt nothing but a longing to be in Justin's arms. Her work no longer seemed to be enough to fill her life.

As she sat in her office late Wednesday afternoon, Ginger stared out the window. In three days she'd studied, talked over, negotiated and approved everything necessary for the running of Howard Management...yet she still saw Justin's face every time she closed her eyes. What the heck was she going to do? The answer seemed obvious. There was no reason she needed to remain in California, so why didn't she hop on the next plane for Colorado?

Her stomach knotted at the thought. She couldn't go back because Justin was there. Justin with his magical kisses and his crazy grin and the gentleness that could wipe away all her defenses. She groaned as the truth hit her. She was scared to death to see him again. He'd been so angry that night at the inn and so cold on the telephone. What if he no longer cared? What if he'd turned to his flirtatious secretary for solace while she was away? What if he'd...

Ginger sat up, swearing at herself. If he'd stopped caring, her problem was solved; she wouldn't have to worry about being in love with him. Nothing would come of her weakness for his kisses if he didn't want to kiss her anymore. Wasn't being free of her fascination with him what she wanted? Sure—that was why she felt like dying at the very thought of him with anyone else.

"Hey, boss, you got a minute to talk?" Ann startled her out of her dark thoughts.

Ginger gave her a smile of gratitude. She definitely preferred solving Ann's problems to dealing with her own. "Sure, what's up?"

"I just wanted to ask you how you feel about my managing the new office." Ann's expression was serious. "I don't want you to think that I'd leave here if you want me to stay. You gave me a good job when I needed it and now... Well, I just hate that all this happened while you were gone."

"I'm thrilled that you'd consider the extra responsibility, Ann. And I can't think of anyone I'd rather trust with it. You and I developed most of our procedures together, so I know you'll keep things right. Of course, I'll miss having you here, but Les and I agree that you're much more than a secretary already, so you deserve a chance to be an office manager." Ginger watched the glow come into Ann's face, remembering the worried single mother who'd come to her what now seemed a lifetime ago.

"You won't be sorry, Ginger. I'll make you glad you gave me this chance."

"I'm already glad. Now tell me what you have planned for your office. You'll be getting the contracts for Enrique's two new buildings, you know. They're out in your area." Ginger leaned back again, listening intently, offering advice and praise as needed. It made for a nice distraction until the shrilling of the telephones drove Ann back to her own desk.

Alone again, Ginger shoved stacks of papers around on her desk, then turned her attention back to the view out her window. She'd enjoyed talking with Ann, but as before, she longed to share her feelings with Justin. She knew he'd understand her pride in her protégé. From that first afternoon, he'd understood her better than anyone she'd ever known, except maybe Dena. She wasn't prepared for the ache of longing that swept through her as she remembered their first meeting in the snow. Suddenly she longed to go home.

Home? Was Willow Run Home now? The very thought stunned her. When had that happened? And what did it mean? Knowing there was only one way to find out, she reached for the phone. She had to get back to Willow Run and face Justin . . . and herself.

Justin paced the waiting area at Stapleton Airport. Where the devil was Ginger's plane? The arrival board listed it as "on time," but it was already ten minutes late and... A swirl of activity near the arrival gate put an end to his impatience and activated the dancing elephants in his belly. Coming to meet her had seemed like a terrific idea when Dena called him last night, but now he wasn't so sure.

But he had to know how she felt about him, he reminded himself as he scanned the emerging passengers, aching to see her in spite of his doubts. He couldn't take much more of this worrying and wondering. The misery he'd tasted the past few days had been more than enough to convince him of that. If she hadn't called to say she was coming back, he'd have booked a flight to California.

He caught a glimpse of her flame-colored hair as she came through the door and his heart rate bounded with excitement. He could see how tired she looked as she paused, frowning as she scanned the crowd. He braced himself for what he might read in her face when she saw him, then called, "Ginger, over here."

Ginger turned, not sure that she'd really heard Justin's voice. Then she saw him, his grin a little tentative as his eyes met hers. "Justin!" Relief and joy swept through her as she hurried toward his open arms. "I didn't know you..."

He didn't need to hear any more. He'd read the answer he sought in her eyes—a longing that matched his own, and the still-burning fire they'd ignited last Saturday night. He took her in his arms and kissed her with a thoroughness that should have satisfied, but only made him long for more.

Dizzy with relief, Ginger clung to him. Her doubts faded as his mouth grew more demanding and she held on tight as blazing desire turned her knees to jelly. Suddenly the prospect of being in love didn't seem quite so frightening. In fact, while he held her, it felt wonderful.

Reality didn't intrude until they'd collected her suitcase and were in his car heading out of town. Justin had brought her up to date on all the latest developments at the inn, Sandy and little Sarah's condition and the fact that Dena claimed Mischief missed Ginger a lot. In return she'd given him a brief résumé of her successful meeting with Enrique and the progress of her branch office. Only then did silence suddenly spread between them. It wasn't the companionable quiet of old friends, but a stillness that fairly hummed with the questions neither of them had asked.

"How are Mom and Dena getting along?" Ginger inquired, ignoring the curiosity she'd read in Justin's gaze. What could she say? Her response to his kiss had told him that she still wanted him, but shared passion didn't give her any clue to what Justin felt. Did he love her? Did he want more than just her happy surrender to the chemistry that flowed so easily between them? Or was she being a fool to even think beyond the present?

"Dena and your mom seem to be doing great. They argue about every little detail of the renovations, but Dena's coming out to the inn now, so I think she's enjoying the battles."

"She's what?" Ginger forgot her emotional confusion for a moment. "But I thought Doc said she was supposed to be very careful about her footing for at least another month. She could fall out there and—"

Justin's chuckle stopped her. "Your mom said you wouldn't approve, but she sticks with Dena every step she takes. Besides, it's Dena's project, Ginger. You can't blame her for wanting to be in the thick of it."

"I suppose you're right." Ginger sighed, surprised to realize that she felt left out. How could so much have happened in the few days she'd been away? She decided to change the subject. "What does Mom think of the inn now that she's had a chance to see what we're doing?"

"She was very impressed when I gave her the guided tour Monday." He grinned at her. "It didn't take me long to figure out where you got that sharp business sense of yours. Your mom is a real whiz at evaluating property."

Ginger stiffened. "You think I'm like my mother?"

"You inherited her business sense. Even Dena says that." He slowed and gave her a curious glance. "I should think you'd be proud. She's showed me before-and-after pictures of their resort in Florida and they did a terrific job on it. If Dena does as well with the inn, she's going to have a winner, that's for sure."

"Mom must have really made an impression." Ginger kept her tone neutral, not comfortable with the comparison to her mother or the admiration she heard in Justin's voice. How could he be so impressed by a woman who always put business first?

"Believe me, you lucked out having a sharp mom and getting Dena's brother for a father." Justin's voice echoed with sadness, reminding her that he'd also grown up feeling close to only one parent—his mother.

"Daddy was the greatest," Ginger agreed. "We used to have so much fun. He always let me work in the drugstore with him even though I must have been a real pain. I used to love it.''

"It's a shame your mother didn't have a chance to get the business back on its feet after he died. But things were real bad in town then, I guess. I know Mom nearly lost the factory at about the same time. You have to admire your mom's guts, though. After fighting so hard and still losing the drugstore, it must have taken a lot of courage to start a risky new business with a new husband.''

Ginger squirmed. "I think she was just glad of an excuse to leave Willow Run.'' Why didn't she remember any of this? she asked herself. If she remembered working in the family drugstore with her dad, why didn't she remember more about her mother being there or the details of the business's failure?

"I don't know about that, Ginger—the way she talks now, I think she kind of misses the place. After all, she grew up here just the way we did.'' Justin studied her, not sure what to think of her tone and the frown that puckered her forehead. Was Ginger thinking that she, too, would be glad to escape Willow Run once again? "Anyway, I do know she's real proud of you and all you've accomplished."

"Sure.'' Ginger closed her eyes, fighting a headache. She didn't want to talk about her mother or think about her own business ventures. It was all too confusing.

"Tired, honey?" Justin reached out to smooth back a wayward tendril of russet hair.

Ginger nodded. "It was a rough three days, trying to get everything caught up so I could get back here.''

"So why don't you take a little nap? We can talk later, when you're feeling better.''

Ginger smiled at him, wondering how he could be so sweet and kind and still confuse her so completely. She closed her eyes, eager to escape into the simple world of dreams.

* * *

Justin sighed as he made the final turn and headed down the hill toward Willow Run. So much for his plans to use the intimacy of the long drive from Denver to really talk to Ginger about their future. She'd fallen asleep the moment she'd curled up against the door and hadn't stirred since.

Had her trip really been that tiring? Or had she spent sleepless nights in the same kind of turmoil that had haunted him? Selfishly, he wanted it to be the latter. At least he hoped she wasn't exhausted because she'd spent her evenings painting the town with some other guy.

Lights were burning at Dena's, but her car wasn't in the drive. Justin pulled up in front and shut off the motor, then leaned over to touch Ginger's slightly parted lips with his own. "You're home, darling," he whispered. She stirred, moaned softly, then slipped her arms around his neck to bring his lips back to hers. It was several heart-stopping moments before he could force himself to break the sensuous contact.

Ginger's lovely eyes opened slowly and she smiled sleepily at him, looking infinitely desirable with her mouth still soft from his kiss. "I was having the most wonderful dream about kissing you," she murmured. "Where are we?"

"That was no dream and you're home." He grinned at her, liking the vulnerability of her expression and the easy way she looked up at him.

She stretched and yawned, still half lying on the seat. As she awoke fully, her expression became almost playful. "Oh, what a fun way to wake up. But you should have done it sooner. I just needed a little nap, then we could have talked."

"I didn't have the heart. You looked so cute all curled up that way. We'll have plenty time to get caught up later."

"I'll be looking forward to it." Ginger forced herself to sit up, suddenly fully realizing that she was back in Willow

Run and that her mother was undoubtedly waiting inside for her. "Will you come in for a while?"

"Maybe just for a minute. I still have to stop by the factory office and see what's happened today." He caught her fingers and lifted them to rub along the roughness of his jaw. "I've missed you, Ginger. I'm very glad you're back."

"I'm glad to be back, too." She swallowed hard, aware that she needed to say more. "And I've missed you a lot, Justin. Everything that happened...well, I wanted to share it with you. It's lonely when you don't have someone special to tell things to."

He touched her cheek with fingers that shook slightly, scarcely trusting the joy her words *someone special* sent through him. "I'll always be here to listen, Ginger. And I'll always want to share what's happening to you."

Before she could respond, the front door opened and Mischief exploded past Dena, to race out to the gate, barking in wild excitement. Ginger rolled her eyes in mock exasperation. "That dog is impossible."

"That dog has missed you almost as much as the rest of us have," Justin corrected her.

Laughing, Ginger jumped from the car and opened the gate to catch the wiggling gray body as Mischief launched herself into her arms. Soft whiskers tickled her as the schnauzer poked her cold nose into her neck, then licked her cheek, whining softly now, as though trying to talk to her.

"Okay, Mischief, so I missed you, too," Ginger whispered, finding her eyes surprisingly damp at this display of affection. "I guess I kind of got used to having you around to talk to."

"Told you she'd grow on you." Justin's grin increased her pulse rate and made her wish even more that she'd stayed awake on the drive here. At the moment she seemed to have a great deal she wanted to say to him.

"Will you two get in here?" Dena called. "I don't need to heat the whole outdoors." Her laughing tone made it clear that she was teasing, but she was impatient to add her greeting to Mischief's.

"Where's Mom?" Ginger asked Dena as Justin carried her suitcase into the house.

"Out at the inn, where else?" There was a note of frustration in Dena's voice. "They started wallpapering in one of the guest rooms today and she couldn't wait to see how it was going to look. She should be back soon."

"Which room?" Ginger shrugged out of her coat. "And what paper did you decide on?"

"The wallpaper was that little blue floral, I think, but I couldn't tell you which room they put it in since I still can't go upstairs." Dena's hug had been more than welcoming, but Ginger caught the gleam of curiosity in her aunt's green eyes when she looked her way. "Does it matter?"

Unwilling to meet Dena's gaze, Ginger bent to pat Mischief. "I was just curious." No way was she going to confess that she'd been thinking of the room in her dream—the dream where she and Justin were making love. "Somehow, I feel like I've been gone weeks instead of days."

"Gives you a slight idea of how I've felt." Dena's tone was tart. "Luckily, Edith got Doc to give his permission for me to visit the inn."

Ginger giggled as she straightened up. "Justin already told me. And I do understand. Just so you're careful."

"I just wish I'd been more careful of the ice on the back steps." Dena sighed. "Come on in and sit down, for heaven's sake. I've got fresh coffee and a plate of cookies to tide you over till dinner. Justin, where are you?"

"Coming." A clatter of footsteps announced that he was coming downstairs after taking Ginger's suitcase to her room. "Did I hear someone mention cookies?"

Dena and Ginger both laughed as they all headed for the kitchen, Mischief bounding ahead of them. Her visit to Seaview faded completely from Ginger's mind as she poured the coffee. She was home now and that was all that mattered.

The next hours flew by and even her mother's arrival didn't change the atmosphere. In fact, as they sat and talked after Justin left, she found herself having difficulty recognizing this smiling and talkative stranger as the mother she remembered. Could there be some sort of magic that came from working on the inn? she asked herself as she went upstairs to unpack and change before dinner. Such a thing never would have occurred to the person she used to be, but now anything seemed possible—especially when she considered the way renovating the inn had changed her own feelings.

"What do you think, dog?" she asked Mischief as the dog settled on the bed beside her suitcase. "Has working on the inn sent me round the bend?"

Mischief's sneeze sounded rather like "yes," while her enthusiastically wagging knob tail made it plain that she approved of the new Ginger. Ginger hugged her. It felt right to be here now and she wasn't eager to look beyond the moment.

Oddly enough, everyone else seemed to be in the same don't-rock-the-boat frame of mind over the next few days. Justin didn't mention her trip to California when they were together and she found it surprisingly easy to ignore as the days passed.

Working with her mother daily proved to be much less painful than she'd expected. They didn't always see eye to eye on the various decorating and renovating projects, but with Dena having the final vote, it was easy to compromise. Her mother even began calling her Ginger instead of Virginia, a pleasant concession.

Ginger was actually sorry Wednesday evening when her mother announced that she was going to fly to Albuquerque, New Mexico, for several days. "What's in Albuquerque?" Ginger asked.

"An old buddy of Evan's. He's visited us several times and he and Evan are discussing more expansion with Geoffrey running the new area. I promised Evan that I'd visit Geoff and see if he's really serious about investing with us."

"You are coming back here, aren't you?" Dena asked.

"Of course. I'll be back either Sunday or Monday. Justin's offered me a ride into Denver with him tomorrow, but I'll have to call and let you know exactly when I'll need to be picked up."

"Justin's going into Denver tomorrow?" Ginger did her best to cover her surprise and disappointment. They'd had almost no time alone together since her return.

Her mother nodded. "I was out at the inn when he came to talk to Robert and he mentioned that one of his interior decorators had just asked him for a consultation on a special order. Since I was planning to fly to Albuquerque, I asked if I could ride along. I hope you don't mind." Her mother's speculative gaze warned Ginger that she'd failed to hide her feelings.

Ginger stiffened. "Why should I mind?"

"I've seen you with Justin, Ginger, and I get the impression that you are...well, more than friends. I wouldn't want you to think I was taking advantage of that." Her mother suddenly seemed very interested in the pattern of the living-room carpet.

"We're old friends, Mom, nothing more." Ginger got to her feet, picking up their coffee cups and carrying them to the kitchen. This was not a conversation she wanted to continue.

Her mother's words followed her. "That's too bad. He's special, Ginger, and I know he cares for you. I think he did even when you were teenagers. If you don't return his feelings, please don't hurt him. He deserves a real chance at happiness and he hasn't had a life of his own since Maria died and left him responsible for both the family and the factory."

Ginger took her time washing the cups. Where did her mother get off saying things like that? Whose side was she on, anyway? Besides, why should she care—she'd left Willow Run behind long ago.

Still, though she found it easy to be angry at her mother's seeming interference in her private business, the words echoed in Ginger's mind long after she was in bed.

Had she been so busy protecting her own fragile heart that she'd overlooked the danger of hurting Justin? But that made no sense—he knew the impossibility of their having a future together as well as she did. They lived in two very different worlds and just because he wanted to make love to her didn't mean he expected anything permanent to come of it.

He needed a wife who'd live here and raise a family, a woman who didn't have a career of her own. A woman like... She felt a stabbing in her chest as she pictured his secretary draped around him. She had no doubt that Cynthia would be delighted to console him once Ginger left Willow Run. And who would console her? she asked herself, shocked by the desolation she felt at the very thought of leaving Justin. What if she couldn't walk away from him?

That question haunted Ginger as the days passed and Justin didn't return from Denver. He called her late Thursday night, sounding excited as he described his business meetings and the new designs he and his decorator friend

Alissa were developing, but Ginger heard only the warmth in his voice as he talked about Alissa.

When he called again Saturday morning, she couldn't hide her disappointment. "You aren't even coming home for the weekend?"

"Alissa has a client coming in this afternoon and since I talked to Edith and she's due in tomorrow, I thought I might as well wait around and give her a ride home."

"Oh." She fought the pain that came from realizing that spending time with her rated so low on his list of priorities.

"You sound kind of down this morning, Ginger. Is there anything going on there that needs my attention?"

Just me, she thought bitterly, but swallowed the words, forcing a cheerful tone. "No, we're getting along fine. You won't know the inn by the time you get back. Half the guest rooms are waiting for furniture now and I think the kitchen will be ready for the new appliances in a couple of weeks."

"Sounds like you're ahead of schedule." Justin's tone was distant. "You must really be cracking the whip."

"No, that's Robert's job. He knows how anxious we are to have everything finished."

"Right. Well, I've got to run. I have a breakfast meeting and I'm already late. See you Sunday night."

Ginger hung up the phone, but stayed in the chair, glaring into space as she scratched Mischief's ears. She didn't even hear Dena until her aunt stopped in front of her.

"Is something wrong?" Dena asked, frowning as she carefully eased herself down on the couch. She used the walker only part of the time now, but her hip was still stiff.

"Justin is bringing Mom back with him tomorrow."

"Don't you want your mother to come back?" Dena's frown deepened. "I thought you and Edith were getting along so well, Ginger."

Ginger shifted nervously under Dena's scrutiny. "Oh, no, it's not that. I'll be glad to have her back."

"Is it Justin, then?"

"Of course not." Ginger sought desperately for an excuse that would satisfy Dena, but none came to mind. "I've just missed him, that's all."

"Does he know that?" Dena's expression changed to one of speculation.

"I suppose so."

"Did you tell him?"

"Well, no, not exactly, but . . ." Ginger studied the mixture of black and silver fur on Mischief's back.

"If you wanted the man to come home, why didn't you tell him how you felt, Ginger?"

Ginger met Dena's gaze, reading the honest concern and love that were so clear in her aunt's face. She sighed. "I can't tell him what I don't know myself, Dena."

Dena shook her head, then got to her feet. "You're too much like your mother, Ginger. When you were little, I told her a million times that she had to learn to let go and really give her love to you, but she never could seem to get the hang of it. She cheated you because she was afraid of being rejected. Loving was always so easy for James and you were such a daddy's girl. Don't make her mistakes, Ginger—Justin's worth the risk."

Chapter Ten

Dena said no more about Justin or Edith through the long day, but Ginger found her aunt's words impossible to ignore. Odd little memories surfaced that afternoon as she worked with Pete and Miles on plans for converting the carriage house to a hot tub facility.

A memory from when she was in the third grade haunted Ginger. She remembered her mother sewing all night to make a daffodil costume for her debut as a dancer—and the way she'd insisted that only Daddy come backstage with her before the recital. Daddy made her feel safe, while her mother... Ginger cringed, suddenly recognizing some of her feelings that long-ago night as guilt. She hadn't wanted to share that exciting, frightening night with her mother, just with Daddy.

Of course her mother hadn't cared. She'd always been too busy with the drugstore and all the other things she did. Ginger had just been another burden loaded on her and... The familiar excuses seemed rather hollow now as she remembered the beauty of her costume and realized how much work it had taken. None of the other flowers in the recital had been so finely dressed.

Other memories followed. Special gifts that she now realized could only have been chosen by her mother, gifts that she'd always treasured and credited to her father. Why hadn't she grasped this at the time, or at least when she was a little older? Why hadn't Mom ever told her that she cared? Hadn't she realized how much Ginger needed to know that her mother loved her, too?

Ginger shook her head, frowning at the plans Pete and Miles had left with her, pushing such errant questions away, cursing Dena for bringing ancient history to mind when she really needed to think about Justin and the future. Her mother simply hadn't wanted a child and all the special things she'd done back then were probably just to assuage her own guilt.

But thinking of Justin didn't make Ginger feel any better. Freely admitting to herself that she'd fallen in love with him hadn't changed anything. His booming business tied him to Willow Run, and her career in property management lay in Seaview. Logic told her that to make a life with Justin she'd have to give up everything she'd worked so hard to create, sacrificing her dreams for his. And how long could love last if she felt resentment at the very thought?

And how long would it take to heal the vast emptiness that opened inside her every time she thought of leaving here and never seeing Justin again? Ginger ground her teeth in frustration. Why did love have to be so darned complicated? Other women just fell in love, got married and were happy. Or never fell in love and still lived wonderful, busy, fulfilled lives doing what they chose. Why had life presented her with such an impossible choice? And how could she ever make a decision?

What really tormented her was that she had only a couple of weeks in which to make up her mind. Once the major renovations were finished, Dena would be well able to handle the rest. In fact, Ginger suspected that her aunt was perfectly capable of doing that now. Except for going up and down long flights of stairs, Dena managed quite well both at home and at the site.

So why didn't she just leave now, before things got even more complicated? The ache in her heart was a clear answer—she had to stay because she couldn't yet bear to leave Justin. She owed him—and herself—some kind of resolution of the feelings that blazed so hot between them. She had to do something.

Ginger kept an eye on the clouds as she packed everything in the huge picnic basket. There was definitely a storm moving in. She could only hope that her mother's plane had landed on time and that she and Justin were nearing home well ahead of the snow that had been forecast for this evening. She frowned, thinking of her careful plans and how easily a storm could cancel them.

"They should be here anytime now," Dena said from the kitchen doorway. "Why don't you go on out to the inn now? It wouldn't do for Justin to catch you here."

Ginger turned to see the broad grin on her aunt's face. "You're enjoying this, aren't you?" she asked, not comfortable with having confided her plans to someone else.

"I approve, if that's what you mean." Dena seemed unfazed by Ginger's bad mood. "I know you two young people need some time alone together and it's obvious from the way things have been going that this is the only way you're going to get it."

"Just tell Justin that I have something to show him and don't let Mom—" Ginger stopped under her aunt's glare.

"Do you really want to run lines with me, Ginger, or are you going to get on your way?"

Ginger closed the picnic basket and reached for her parka. "I'm out of here. Give Mom my love and tell her I'm glad she's back."

"You can tell her yourself…later." Dena followed her to the back door. "Just have fun, Ginger. You're much too serious these days."

Ginger grinned up at her before she got in her car. "Life is serious, Aunt Dena—didn't anyone ever tell you that?"

"Life is to be lived, Ginger, and having fun is a part of living. Don't cheat yourself out of all the good moments just because you're afraid of getting hurt."

Ginger opened her mouth to protest that she wasn't afraid of anything, but Dena was already closing the door to keep Mischief inside. She climbed into the sports car. Just what she needed, a gimpy-hipped Cupid hard at work messing in her life. Ginger waved to Dena as she backed out of the driveway, then sighed. Dena couldn't make things any worse than she had herself.

The air was already noticeably colder when she parked outside the inn. Maybe there would be a blizzard after Justin arrived and they'd be marooned here. Justin could carry her up to the special room from her dream and … Ginger shook her head at her foolish romantic fantasy.

More than likely, they'd just have to leave early if the snow was heavy. Besides, the beautiful brass bed from her dream hadn't been delivered yet and the heat wasn't turned on upstairs, so they'd probably freeze anywhere except right in front of the big fireplace. Not to mention the possibility that Justin might have better things to do with his time after having spent a long weekend with Alissa.

Doubt swelled inside her, making her wonder if she shouldn't just forget the whole crazy plan. Then she remembered that Dena would be waiting with all sorts of questions. Shivering, she went inside and began setting up for her surprise party.

Chili simmered fragrantly in Dena's crockpot while she lit the fire she'd laid this morning and set out the candles. Next she carried the corn bread to the kitchen where she could heat it in the newly installed microwave oven. Salads and wine went in the small refrigerator the crews had been using for their lunches. The small, heart-shaped chocolate cake that Dena had baked stayed in the basket.

Bringing in the blankets and cushions took another few minutes, then everything was ready. Ginger surveyed the scene, remembering the last time she'd seen it like this—the Saturday before her trip to Seaview. Though it had been only a day over two weeks, she felt as though a century had passed.

What if Justin took one look at the scene and turned around and walked out? She wouldn't exactly blame him, but she wasn't sure she could bear the rejection. Yet that was pretty much what she'd done that night. Instead of facing his anger and talking about what was happening between them, she'd fled all the way to Seaview.

And what if he stayed? What if he looked around and assumed that she wanted to continue the seduction he'd begun that night? The wild quivering deep inside made it clear that a part of her was more than ready to surrender to her love for him. But the cautious side of her knew that making love now would only complicate their already complicated relationship.

"Oh, Dena, I could be making a really big mistake," she murmured to the silent room, shivering as she listened to the rising wind wailing around the corners. Then, above the sound of the wind, she heard a car door slam. Justin had arrived.

Justin pulled his topcoat tighter around him, frowning at the inn. Ginger's car was here, but the place looked deserted. Not that anyone would be working on Sunday afternoon, but... Then he saw the flickering reflection of firelight on the windows and his heart did a slow flip-flop. Almost afraid to believe what he was seeing, he swallowed hard as he ran up the stairs.

Ginger stood just inside the door, her auburn curls glowing ruddy in the light of the flames that blazed on the hearth. Candles flickered in the breeze as he closed the door and for a moment all he could think about was the last time they'd been alone here like this. If he closed his eyes, he knew he'd see her as she'd been in the passionate moments before he'd found out she was leaving town. Remembering just how that evening had ended cooled the flames of excitement that had been building inside him ever since Dena had sent him out here.

Ginger watched the expressions that moved over Justin's face. She saw anticipation as he stepped inside... then a blazing glow of excitement and love when he saw the blankets spread in front of the fire... then suddenly nothing. She felt a chill as she realized that he'd masked his feelings, shutting her out.

"Welcome home, Justin." Those were the first words that came into her mind. "I hope you're in the mood for a surprise picnic."

Caution kept him from admitting just how much he was in the mood for a private picnic with her. "What's the occasion?"

"Just what I said. I wanted to give you a special welcome home." Ginger had to fight to keep her voice from shaking and her smile felt pasted on. This wasn't the way it was supposed to happen. She needed to be in Justin's arms, to feel his lips on hers, to know that he hadn't stopped wanting her.

Her smile was beginning to fade and even in the poor light Justin could see the sheen of tears sparkling in her beautiful eyes. His doubts vanished like snowflakes caught on the tongue. In two strides, he crossed the few feet separating them and pulled her into his arms. She felt so right there, the heat of her body matching the fire she'd ignited inside him.

"Now I'm home," he whispered as his lips found hers.

The change came so swiftly she scarcely had time to recognize the love blazing from his eyes before she was wrapped in his embrace, her eyes closing as she lifted her lips to welcome his. She pressed herself into the hard length of his body, glorying in the dizzy waves of desire that rippled through her. Nothing mattered but tangling her fingers in the crisp, cold curls on the nape of his neck as she returned his hungry kiss with matching passion.

Justin lost himself in the sweetness of her mouth and the heated softness of her body, feeling the shattering impact of his own too-long-denied desire for her. No woman had ever ignited this mind-stealing fire in him before, and after a few moments the very wildness of his need for her forced him back to sanity. Slowly, painfully, he eased his devouring kiss before he claimed the rest of her with equal hunger.

"I've missed you so much, Ginger," he whispered as he tasted each corner of her luscious mouth, then moved on to explore her eyelids and her cheeks with his lips. "I was beginning to think we'd never have a moment alone again."

"That's why I thought we needed another picnic." Ginger clung to him, not sure that her knees would support her. How could one kiss turn her very bones to jelly and leave her aching for more? Could love truly be so potent or had she finally slipped into madness? It was frightening to feel so vulnerable, so at the mercy of another person's emotions, yet she had no defenses when she was near him.

Justin heard the quiver in her voice and felt Ginger trembling against him. For a moment he thought that she was overcome with desire, then he recognized the confusion in her face and cursed himself for allowing his own passion to overwhelm his control. One kiss was all it took for him to be sure of his feelings, but Ginger obviously needed more.

Could independent Ginger be afraid of her own feelings? It seemed unlikely, yet what else could make her pull away? He dropped a casual kiss on the tip of Ginger's nose and stepped back slightly, keeping just one arm around her. He sniffed the air, suddenly aware of a mouth-watering aroma. "So what smells so good?"

Ginger drew in a deep breath, caught between relief and disappointment as she regained control of her emotions. The violence of her love for him frightened and excited her at the same time and, in spite of her fear, she ached to explore the new feelings he'd ignited. "The chili, I guess. I hope you're hungry."

He was starved for her kisses, but he forced that need aside. "I sure am. I had lunch early and we were afraid to stop for anything on the way home, with that cold front coming in behind us."

"When it got so cloudy, I was afraid you wouldn't make it." Ginger spoke to keep the silence at bay, but the words couldn't convey the feelings that coursed through her as they walked to the hearth. In spite of her doubts and fears, her love flowed to him with every touch and glance. Never had she felt so open and vulnerable.

"If I'd known this was waiting, I'd have been here sooner." He looked into her eyes and felt the impact of the love he saw there, then forced himself to look away, buying time to get his own desire under control. "What can I do to help with this feast?"

Working together to get the food ready made it easy to talk about the time they'd spent apart. Justin had questions about the progress on the inn's renovations and once she'd given him the details, Ginger felt free to ask if he'd been successful in Denver. She didn't mention Alissa.

"Remarkably. Everything seems to be taking off at once. If this keeps up, I may be spending the next few months planning renovations of my own. I need to double my production just to keep up with the orders I have now, and with your mother promoting my new line—"

"Mom?" Ginger nearly choked on a bite of chili. "When did she get involved?"

"I told you she called me from Albuquerque on Friday. Well, she wanted some details of price and production time on the rustic line. Seems this friend she was visiting owns a couple of dude ranches—one near Santa Fe, the other in southern New Mexico somewhere. Anyway, she told him about the line and he was very interested. I'll be going down there next Tuesday or Wednesday with samples and projections."

"That's fantastic, Justin." She tried hard for enthusiasm, but it wasn't easy to be happy about his leaving again on business when she knew their time together would be ending all too soon. "I had no idea Mom was such a good saleswoman."

"She's promised to do the same in Florida, too. She already told me she'd like to take the brochures for my antique-style Victorians and now she wants pictures of the new rustic prototypes, as well. She knows the owners of several rustic-style fishing resorts that she's sure would be very interested in those designs."

"At the rate you're going, you won't be able to expand fast enough to fill all the orders." And he'd be far too busy to even think about falling in love.

"That's what Alissa said, only she suggested that I look around the area for another factory, one that I could merge with or sell a manufacturing franchise to." Justin helped himself to more corn bread and refilled his chili bowl, though he scarcely seemed aware of what he was doing.

A chill chased down Ginger's spine at his mention of Alissa. The woman probably wanted him to headquarter in Denver so he'd be close to her. She had no trouble picturing a statuesque blonde "helping" him with his expansion while she seduced him into marriage. Justin was so vulnerable it would be easy to win his heart.

Inspiration struck. "What about going out of state for a factory?" Ginger swallowed a giggle of pure joy as the plan she'd imagined for Alissa suddenly offered her a possible solution to her own long-distance romance dilemma. "I have a lot of friends in California real estate. I could make a couple of calls and see what they could find for you on the coast."

"California?" Justin set down his food, the knot in his stomach making swallowing anything else impossible. Every time he even thought about Alissa's suggestions of vast expansion he lost his appetite. But when he looked at Ginger he could see the changes in her face. He'd sensed her reservations earlier; now her eyes were glowing with excitement.

"There might even be some possibilities in Seaview. We have a pretty extensive industrial district, so I'm sure..." She reined in her enthusiasm as she realized that he wasn't smiling. "Of course, if you're not interested?"

"Of course I'm interested, Ginger. It's just that all this has happened so quickly. Three years ago I was still worrying about keeping McGovern Fine Furnishings in the black. Now..."

"Now the sky's the limit. That's the way my company took off. It's scary and exciting and wonderful." Ginger leaned closer, wanting to share her enthusiasm with him, yet sensing some deep reservations behind his caution.

Her eagerness and belief in him were irresistible. Justin pulled her into his arms. "Guess I'm just a small-town guy at heart," he confided. "I don't quite trust all this sudden good fortune."

"It's not really sudden, you know," Ginger whispered as she traced the contours of his face with gentle fingers. "You've been paying your dues ever since you came back here to take over. It's just finally paying off." She nibbled on his ear. "Don't you want to be a furniture mogul?"

"Right now, it doesn't seem important at all." He turned his head to capture her lips, delving into her sweetness, losing himself in the magic fire that seemed always to lie just beneath the surface of their relationship, waiting to consume them.

All other thoughts vanished from Ginger's mind as the soaring passion flooded through her body, melding her to him. She slipped her hands inside his shirt to explore his back and shoulders. She wanted to touch every inch of him, to bury her fingers in the tangled mat of black curls that covered his chest, to feel his bare skin burning against hers as—

The shrill ringing of the phone shattered the spell. Justin tightened his arms for a moment, then groaned as he lifted his lips from hers. "Who the hell—?"

"Dena's the only one who knew we were going to be here." Ginger got to her feet slowly, not sure her dizzy desire would allow her to walk. She answered without enthusiasm.

"Hello, Ginger, is Justin there? Dena said you were having a special dinner...."

Ginger recognized Holly's voice in spite of the strain in it. "He sure is, just one second." She felt Justin's supportive arm around her waist even before she handed the receiver to him.

His conversation was brief, but Ginger felt the joy and warmth draining away even before he hung up. His face was grim as he looked down at her. "We've got to get back to town. There was a fire at the movie theater tonight and they need blood donors at the hospital."

A chill spread through her. "Was anyone seriously hurt?"

"Holly didn't think so, but Michael called from the hospital. He was at the theater and he's fine. He'd already given blood and since we're the same type, he figured I could do the same." His slight grin didn't relieve the worry in his eyes. "Popular blood type, you know."

Ginger took a deep breath and forced herself to move away from his supportive embrace. "You go on ahead. I'll take care of things here, then meet you at the hospital. I don't know what my blood type is, but if they need some, I'd be glad to contribute."

"I hate to leave." Justin's kiss was filled with longing. "It seems like we'd just begun to..."

"There'll be other nights," Ginger promised, hoping that she was right. The end of her work on the inn renovations now loomed ominously close, but if she could actually find a factory site in Seaview... The image of what it would be like to have Justin living in California made it easy to smile and wave as he left her alone with the wailing wind and the remains of their picnic.

Ginger packed everything away quickly, then put out the fire she'd lit with such high hopes and dreams. It took two trips through the swirling snow to get everything in the car and she was shivering as she locked up. Seaview seemed far away as she started down the road for home. Still, the possibility that Justin could relocate there lifted her spirits. Finally there was a real chance that they could build a life together, and she meant to make it work even if she had to build the damned factory there herself.

Laughing at her own determination, she headed for Dena's to drop off the food before she went to the hospital. Her romantic picnic might have been scuttled, but she could still spend what was left of the evening with Justin.

* * *

By noon on Monday, Ginger had called four realtor friends in the Seaview area and given them all the information she'd gleaned from her purposely casual conversation with Justin while they waited to give blood. All four had promised to scout for possible locations and get back to her as soon as possible.

Ginger smiled to herself as she hung up after the final call. If they found something soon enough, maybe Justin would consider making the drive to Seaview with her when she went home. She could hardly wait to see his face when she surprised him with the good news that she'd located the perfect site for him to look at. That settled, she headed for the inn to catch up with Dena and her mother, who'd gone out earlier.

The day flew by as she and Dena showed her mother all that had been accomplished in her absence. Ginger had no time to think of anything besides the inn until late afternoon as she and her mother drove home after their second visit to the site.

"I want to thank you for what you're doing to help Justin," Ginger began. "His business is really taking off and the leads you're giving him will help him expand in a lot of new markets."

"He has a good product to offer and one that most of the bigger manufacturers can't match. His small facility here and his highly skilled work force enable him to do specialty work that's hard to find these days."

Her mother's enthusiasm pricked Ginger's curiosity. "You two really seem to get along well."

Her mother leaned back and closed her eyes. "I guess in some ways he reminds me of your father, Ginger. He's so strong and complete within himself. It's great that his business is doing well. But unlike so many men, that's not all that matters to him. He'd be the same man even if it failed."

"I don't think there's a chance of that. He's talking about expanding and..." Ginger let it trail off, suddenly realizing that she didn't want to talk to her mother about Justin's plans and dreams. Instead, her thoughts turned to her father and the past. "Why didn't you ever tell me the drugstore was in trouble, Mom?"

"I did try, Ginger, but you wouldn't listen. You just kept telling me that it was my fault, that if your father had lived he would have saved the business." Her gaze was sad. "He was your hero— I couldn't destroy that image. You had little enough to hold on to after he died."

Memories flooded into her mind. Suddenly she could see how dingy and run-down the drugstore had been those last years. She remembered her father's worried gaze as he opened each morning and the lines in his face as he closed up each night. Ginger slowed, wanting to finish the discussion before she pulled into Dena's driveway. "Why didn't you sell out sooner?"

"James kept hoping that he could turn the place around, that things would get better. After he died, it was too late. No one wanted the place."

"You would have sold it sooner, wouldn't you?"

Her mother nodded. "I guess I should have insisted, but I just wanted him to be happy."

"But you were right...maybe about a lot more things than I realized." It hurt to say the words, but she had to. She owed her mother some honesty after all these years.

"Loving someone makes being right unimportant, Ginger. In fact, when you truly love, very little else matters. Please always remember that. Otherwise, you'll never really find the happiness you deserve." Her mother looked as though she'd like to say more, but they were already at Dena's and they could both hear Mischief's eager bark of welcome as Dena opened the door for them.

* * *

Ginger found the next few days frustrating. In spite of what had happened between them before Holly's call interrupted their picnic at the inn, she didn't see Justin again before he left Wednesday to keep his business appointment in Albuquerque.

When he called, Justin sounded disappointed not to be spending time with her, yet she sensed a chasm growing between them and she wasn't sure how to bridge it. She'd let him know how she felt when she arranged their picnic. Now she wondered if her efforts had come too late. She ached to go by the factory and talk to him, but her fear of rejection was too strong.

To avoid dwelling on her fear that she might be losing Justin, Ginger turned her attention to her relationship with her mother. After their discussion about the past, she could no longer think of her mother as the cold and unloving parent she'd always pictured.

As she mentally replayed everything she'd recently learned about her mother, more and more memories surfaced. By Wednesday evening when Dena went out to a special bridge dinner leaving the two of them alone, she could bear it no longer. It was time to have another talk with her mother.

She opened with the question that had tortured her for years. "What happened when I was born, Mom? I mean, I feel like we've gotten close now, so why did I always feel like you never wanted me?"

"Ginger, I wanted you desperately, but things got very rocky financially about the time you were born, so I couldn't stay home with you the way I'd planned. That's why Dena took care of you."

"You really wanted to be with me?" A longing to believe filled Ginger.

"Of course I did. Why do you find that so hard to believe?"

Ginger hesitated a moment, then plunged on. "I just never remember you being around much. It seemed like everything else was more important to you than I was."

Her mother flinched at the implied accusation, but her tone held only sadness, not anger. "You didn't want me around, Ginger. You told me so, often enough. 'Daddy do it,' or 'Dena fix.' Those were your favorite words from the time you started to talk."

"I..." Ginger couldn't make any excuse.

"It was my fault for allowing them to spend so much time with you, but they were the ones who knew how to care for a baby. I was all thumbs, so I did what I felt competent doing. When I wasn't working at the drugstore, I kept books for other people for extra money. By the time we were finally out of debt, I'd lost touch with you and I didn't know how to get your love back."

"But you wanted it—my love, I mean?"

"Of course I did. I tried to tell you, but you wouldn't listen. I tried to show you, but no matter what I did, it was never enough. When James died we needed each other so much, but there wasn't room in your heart for me. That's why I didn't try to keep you with me in Florida, Ginger. You'd chosen Dena, so I couldn't put my longing to have you before your need to be safe here with her."

"Why didn't you tell me?" Pain made her words rough and accusing and she couldn't stop the tears that were flowing down her cheeks. "Why didn't you ever just tell me that you loved me, that you wanted me?"

"I guess I didn't know how. And I really didn't think it mattered to you." The tears in her mother's eyes made it clear just how deeply she, too, had been hurt.

Ginger felt the tearing inside as all the pain and guilt were ripped from her heart. She threw herself into her mother's arms, clinging to her as they both sobbed. "It did matter,

Mom," she whispered. "It still matters because I do love you."

They held each other until Mischief came racing in, her bright eyes filled with worry. As they reassured the dog, Ginger felt more at peace than she had in years. She and her mother had found their way back to each other, so perhaps there was hope for her and Justin, too. There had to be!

Chapter Eleven

Thursday morning Ginger got the call from California for which she'd been waiting. Toby Partridge had found a furniture factory in Seaview whose owner was headed for bankruptcy court. Ginger's fingers shook as she took down all the information.

"There's only one thing, Ginger," Toby warned. "This one isn't going to be available long. If your friend waits past Monday to make an offer, the place could be gone. It's prime and the price is outstanding for this area."

"I'll tell him Toby, but I just know he's going to want the place as soon as he hears about it. It's perfect."

Ginger called the factory immediately, hoping to learn when Justin would return. Holly answered. "I talked to him last night and he wasn't sure. He thought he might stay over in Denver tonight. It seems that Alissa has something she wants to show him."

"Damn." Ginger fought back the rising flames of jealousy. She had no doubt that Alissa had also found a property for Justin. "If you hear from him again, will you please ask him to call me, Holly? I really need to talk to him."

Ginger glared off into space as she replaced the receiver. What if she was too late? Why hadn't she trusted her feelings for Justin enough to talk to him about her plans before he left? It shattered her to realize that not taking risks might be the biggest risk of all.

Justin stood in the silent and empty office staring at the note Holly had left on his desk and wondering why Ginger had been trying to get in touch with him. Since it was just a little after eight, he picked up the phone and dialed Dena's familiar number, suddenly glad that he hadn't stayed over in Denver. Once he'd made his decision on the drive up from Albuquerque, there'd been no reason not to come home.

The moment he heard Ginger's voice on the phone, he felt a surge of excitement. "Hiya, gorgeous," he said. "What's up?"

"Justin." Just hearing his voice took her breath away. "Where are you?"

"At the factory. I just got into town and stopped by to drop off some papers. There was a note on my desk saying you wanted me to call. Has something happened?"

Ginger took a deep breath, then let it out slowly. She couldn't tell him on the phone. She had to be in his arms when she announced that she'd found the solution to all their problems. Besides, the time for caution and logic was past. Now she needed to take the most important risk of her life.

Hope made her breathless. "Remember that dessert we didn't eat last Sunday night? Well, I kept it and I think we should go to the inn and pick up where we left off. What do you think?"

"That's the best offer I've had since last Sunday. I can be there in ten minutes."

"See you then." Ginger broke the connection, then just sat still, a mixture of anticipation and anxiety paralyzing her. It had to work out, she told herself. Everything had to turn out right for them this time.

Justin's car was already parked near the door when she pulled up and as she lifted the cake and thermos of coffee from the seat, she caught the scent of burning pine. He'd started a fire—in the fireplace as well as in her heart. It seemed like a good omen.

Justin opened the heavy door for her, sweeping her into his arms the moment she stepped inside. "The cake," she warned, trying not to drop the pan. Then her worry faded as his lips found hers.

"You're the only dessert I need." Justin moved his lips over her cool cheeks, heating them and stoking the flames of his own desire. How could he have stayed away from her for so long when just touching her made him ache with love? She had to agree to stay with him, to be his wife. They were meant to be.

Ginger was only dimly aware of being led across the cold room to the nest of blankets Justin had spread before the fire. Justin took the pan and thermos, then her coat before he gently eased her down on the blankets. "My love," he whispered, his lips creating a wonderful new chaos of desire as they trailed down the side of her neck and touched the pulse at the base of her throat. "I never want to be away from you again."

Joy exploded through her. "Oh, Justin, that's what I want, too. I love you." The words came easily and filled her with pleasure at having said them.

His lips returned to hers as his hands began a tender exploration that left shivers of delight in its wake. Ginger unbuttoned his shirt and pushed it aside, nestling her cheek against the wiry black curls on his chest, then turned her head to kiss the soft skin beneath. His love surrounded her and she ached to become his completely, to forget her doubts and questions and surrender to the pulsing drumbeat of her own desire.

Justin groaned, fighting the intensity of his need to claim her, to make her his own for all time. "If we don't slow down, I'm never going to be able to stop, Ginger," he warned, moving away a few inches. "Maybe I'm an old-fashioned guy, but I think we should talk before we make love, don't you?"

Ginger shivered as the night air moved over her partially uncovered breasts. She wanted to pull him back, to rub against him until she forgot everything but the magic of loving him, but she knew he was right. Surrendering to their passion would be sweeter once they'd committed themselves to a future together.

Justin looked into her eyes, drawing strength from the love burning there. "I realized while I was away that I love you, Ginger, and I can't let you disappear from my life without a fight. I want you here and now. But I want you forever, too. It's as simple as that."

Ginger caught her breath at the decisiveness of his words and the depth of commitment they offered. She tried to match his honesty. "I—I feel the same way, Justin. But I've been afraid. I couldn't bear to make love with you and then walk away, yet I knew that I'd never be able to fit into your world here."

Justin kissed her so he wouldn't have to hear about her doubts. "But you do belong here, Ginger, don't you realize that now? The Willow Run Inn is as much your creation as Dena's and you should be a part of its continuing growth and expansion. You know as well as I do that even if Dena recovers completely, she'll need help to manage it and..."

Ginger shook her head, stopping his words with a finger to his lips. "I found a better solution, Justin. The real answer." She quickly explained about her calls to California and the property that Toby Partridge had found for him, ending, "I have all the information for you. I thought we could go to California together and you could look the property over, but I just know it will be perfect for your expansion."

Ginger suddenly became aware of a change in Justin's face. Though he hadn't moved, she sensed a withdrawal and the room seemed colder than before. What was wrong? Had she taken too much for granted? Could he have already taken the property Alissa had found for him? She hurried on. "I know you were talking about a Denver factory, but think of all the new markets you could develop in California. This site would be so much more profitable in the long run and then we could be together in Seaview."

"In Seaview, but not in Willow Run." Justin's voice was soft and his expression unreadable, but Ginger felt the chill growing around her.

"We could be together in both places, Justin. Don't you see, we'd have it all, everything we ever wanted. My business is growing and so is yours and this way we'd have each other, too."

"Just no real home, no roots, no place to raise a family, right?" Justin tried not to let the bitterness show, but he couldn't hide his pain. "I'm sure your business would thrive and so would mine, but what about us, Ginger? Where would our marriage fit in? Scheduled appointments? Vacations?"

The angry disappointment in his voice tore at her, breaking through the shock his words had given her. "It wouldn't be like that, Justin! I promise, you'd come first."

"Like I do now? Ginger, I made a decision on the way home from Albuquerque. I realized that I don't want my business to expand to Denver or anywhere else. I don't want to end up heading a huge business where I don't know the people who work for me or have a hand in the products we

turn out. I'm happy here. I love the new designs and I want
to do more, but on a small scale. If I expand, it'll be here
where I can help the local economy and make Willow Run
an even better place to live."

"You don't want to grow or change." Desperation turned
to anger as she realized she was losing him. "You're afraid
of leaving here, Justin, that's all. You'll get over it." She had
to make him see that together they could conquer anything.

"No, Ginger, I'm not afraid. I just don't want to trade the
things that make me happy for something that won't."

"You mean something like me?" Tears filled her eyes and
spilled over her cheeks as the truth finally penetrated her
mind. "You want me here as a good little housewife and
mother or not at all. Justin, I can't give up everything. I
can't live the kind of life you're asking me to. I wish I could,
but I just . . ." She couldn't go on. Her heart was breaking
as all the love that had filled it shattered under the impact
of reality. "It would never work."

Justin looked deep into her eyes, seeking some sign that
her words were just empty protests brought on by her fear
of commitment, but instead he read the truth. His love
wasn't enough for Ginger. His willingness to devote his life
to making her happy meant nothing if she had to give up her
business.

Hurt, angry and frustrated, Justin pulled her into his
arms, seeking her mouth once more. Her whimper told him
that he was bruising her lips with his kiss, but he couldn't
help himself. All his love boiled over as he sought to claim
her forever. To love her until she realized she belonged in his
arms.

For a heartbeat, Ginger fought the violent hunger unleashed by Justin's kiss, then she surrendered to her need to
love him. Right or wrong, doomed or not, she did love him

with all her heart and she wanted desperately to make him give their love a chance.

Suddenly Justin thrust her away and scrambled to his feet. "No, Ginger," he growled. "Not like this, not knowing that my love means so little to you."

He was gone before she could fight her way through the dazzling waves of passion his kiss had sent pulsing inside her. She started to get up, then settled back in the blankets, shivering from a cold that had nothing to do with temperature. Her dreams of love ebbed, leaving hollow emptiness where her heart had been—where Justin had been.

The next week proved to be the longest of her life. She got up each day and did what was required—helping Dena, supervising the final stages of the renovations, visiting with Sandy, driving her mother into Denver to catch the plane—but only a part of her was alive.

Her heart was in suspended animation just waiting for a phone call, a chance to talk to Justin, but she neither saw nor heard from him. When Dena asked questions about his absence, Ginger said only that he was busy with his expansion plans. But deep down, she knew she was fooling no one. She was totally miserable without him and the prospect of returning to Seaview did nothing to lift her spirits.

Friday, Dena made her way up to the second floor of the inn to check the guest rooms in person for the first time. As Ginger watched her walking down the hall, pausing at each doorway, she knew that Dena no longer needed her. Her aunt could easily handle the remaining preparations for opening the inn. It was time for Ginger to take her broken heart back to California to heal.

"Why, Ginger?" Dena asked as they rode back to town. "Why are you so set on going back to Seaview right now?"

"You don't need me anymore. You can drive, the inn is progressing on schedule and I . . ." She'd meant to say that she had a business of her own to run, but memories of Justin choked off the words.

"And you are running away from Justin." Dena finished the sentence her own way. "Can't you see he loves you?"

For a moment she considered not answering, but the pain of Dena's accusation made her want to tell the real story. "I'm not running away, Dena. I was ready to give him my love, but he doesn't want me unless I'm willing to give up everything and settle in Willow Run."

"Would that be so terrible, Ginger?"

"I've worked very hard to build my management company, Dena. Why should I have to walk away from it? I love what I do and I'm good at it. I was willing to compromise. I even had my friend Toby Partridge find a possible factory in Seaview for Justin's expansion. I thought if part of his business was in California, we could share everything, have the best of both worlds."

"And he wouldn't consider it?" Dena's frown made her feel a little better. At least Dena could see that she wasn't the one at fault.

"He accused me of putting my business before him."

"Were you?"

"Of course not. I love him, but I can't just sell everything to Les and become a housewife. I'd hate it, Dena. He doesn't want me, he wants someone like Sandy. She's happy and I envy that, but I can't be like her."

Dena nodded. "Did you tell him that?"

"He didn't give me a chance." Ginger sighed. "He was hurt and angry when he left the inn and I haven't talked to him since. Which is probably for the best, anyway. All we've done is hurt each other. Just loving each other obviously isn't enough."

"You're going to give up so easily? If he was a client you were trying to sign, I doubt that you'd be so willing to walk away."

"But he's not a client and it hurts too much to be near him. I have to face the fact that it's over, so I'm going home next week."

Dena looked as though she'd like to argue, but after a moment she just reached out and patted Ginger's hand. "I'll miss you, you know. Mischief and I have gotten very used to having you around."

"I'll miss you and the maniacal mutt, too." Ginger blinked back tears as a sharp pain knifed through her. How could she have let herself become so dependent on Dena's loving friendship? And what would she do alone in Seaview?

Though Dena offered no more comments or arguments against her leaving, Ginger found herself torn with ambivalence as she began packing. She felt drawn to the inn and all the memories she and Justin had created there. Finally, on Sunday afternoon, she drove out to the building for one last visit, taking only Mischief for company.

"What do you think, dog?" she asked as she followed the busy schnauzer around the sunlit building, soaking up the feeling of spring without noticing the dark clouds rising over the nearby mountains. "Does this place look like it'll be a success?"

Mischief barked an answer, then turned her attention to a thick bush near a fallen log. Ginger slowed, suddenly aware that she was very much alone out here. "What's up, Mischief?" she asked, feeling slightly foolish to be caught talking to a dog. "Is someone there?"

Mischief's stubby tail began to wag as a white poodle came prancing out to greet her. Ginger relaxed, recognizing him as belonging to the Halls, a couple who lived in a cabin just over the hill. She laughed as the two dogs greeted each other then disappeared around the log together. "Don't get lost," she called after Mischief, then shook her head. She'd obviously been here too long if she expected the dog to heed her warning.

Feeling lonely without Mischief's company, Ginger went inside. The rooms were haunted with images of Justin—all the laughter, the shared dreams, that first night when he'd saved her from the falling bootjack, their spectacular kisses... Sobs shook her. How could she ever forget the magic they'd shared? Going to Seaview wouldn't make the hurt go away.

They had to talk. She ached with the need to see him just once more, and there was no better place than this. She picked up the phone and dialed his number before she could change her mind. If there was any chance for them at all, she'd gladly risk her heart once more.

Justin drove slowly along the narrow road, still not sure what he was going to say, but positive that he had to say something. He couldn't let her go. The dark clouds now moving over the sun echoed his mood since Thursday night and made it clear that life without the glow of Ginger's company really wasn't worth living.

Thank God she'd called. He only hoped that meant she'd been just as miserable as he had. If she'd come to her senses about staying here... A rumble of thunder shook the air and the first gust of wind whipped the trees. He shivered, remembering what Dena had told him when he'd called her yesterday.

Was he wrong to want to keep his life the way it was? Had Ginger been right to accuse him of being afraid to leave Willow Run? Could they find a compromise that would satisfy them both? Dena had read him Ginger's notes about the factory in Seaview and he'd called her real estate man out there yesterday afternoon. The man had assured him the factory was still on the market.

Justin's stomach knotted. He really wasn't sure whether expanding to California would be the right thing to do. Damn it, he wasn't sure about anything except his need to be with Ginger, to hold her and tell her that he loved her.

The thunder crashed again as he parked beside her car. It was definitely going to storm.

He heard her voice as soon as he got out of the car. She was calling Mischief and she sounded worried. He followed the sound and found her behind the inn. "Lose something?" he asked, taking her in his arms.

Ginger leaned against him, glorying in the sensation of having his arms around her, drinking in his special scent hungrily. Suddenly she was sure she could never let him go. "It's Mischief. Dena told me she's scared to death of thunder and I can't find her."

"When did you see her last?" Justin's arms tightened. She felt so right pressed against him, needing him, wanting him. There had to be a way. Hell, he'd move to Seaview if that was what it took. Willow Run couldn't be home without Ginger.

"She was with the Halls' little poodle. I thought they'd just play around in the area, like they usually do, but she didn't come when I called her."

"Maybe she's at the Halls'. Why don't you go in and call them?"

Ginger clung to him for a moment longer, then stepped back. "I already called and the dogs aren't there, either." She shivered even in her parka. "Mrs. Hall is frantic. Jo-Jo got out of their backyard and her husband has been looking for him for nearly an hour. Where could they be?"

"We'll find them," Justin assured her, hoping that his voice didn't betray his own growing uneasiness. He'd felt the change in the wind, the sharpening cold. By nightfall the rain could very well change to snow. "They can't have gone far. Which way were they headed, do you remember?"

"Around this fallen log. I went inside after that and . . ." Ginger swallowed a sob as she rounded the log. "Oh, Justin, it would break Dena's heart if something happened to Mischief. And mine, too. She's—"

Justin stopped her words with a light kiss. "Stop worrying. I think I know where she went. See those tracks?" He pointed to some scuff marks in the soft soil. "They were probably following the deer that use this trail."

"Do you really think we can find them?" Ginger wanted to believe him, but the wooded flanks of the mountain seemed to rise endlessly and Mischief, despite her noisy bravado, would be defenseless against the wilderness.

"There's only one way to find out." Justin gave her a quick hug. "But we'd better hurry before the storm hits. I have a hunch it's going to be a bad one."

The search seemed endless. Even as she shouted Mischief's name, Ginger's mind filled with horrible possibilities. Her own carelessness haunted her. She'd lost the dog so quickly, so easily—she couldn't help seeing the similarities to what had happened between her and Justin. She'd been just as careless with their love for each other.

The first spatters of rain began to fall and as the day darkened around them, Ginger knew they couldn't go on much longer. Then, at last, she caught a distant sound. She stopped, listening intently until she heard it again. "Justin," she shouted, realizing that he'd vanished into the shadows. "Justin, I hear Mischief!"

"This way, Ginger." Justin appeared from behind a thick pine trunk several feet off the narrow track they'd been following. "I think she's somewhere over here."

Even with Mischief's shrill bark as a guide, they nearly missed spotting the worried schnauzer as she paced beside a crevice in the rocky mountainside. A whimper came from

he narrow fissure. "Jo-Jo," Ginger gasped, peering down
nto the dark hole as he hugged Mischief. The white poodle
ooked up at her, whining loudly now. "How did you get in
here?"

"More important, how do we get him out?" Justin asked,
kneeling on the rock behind her.

"If you hold on to me, I think I can reach him," Ginger
eplied, shoving Mischief behind her, then leaning over the
edge of the crevice and extending her arms toward the little
dog.

Justin's hands tightened around her waist, comfortingly
warm and protective as she slid forward over the lip of the
damp rock. It was a tight squeeze as she moved further
down, and she felt a sharp edge of stone cutting into her
back as she closed her hands around the wiggly, wet body.
"Got him!"

Within moments, the two dogs were happily greeting each
other while Justin took Ginger in his arms. He snuggled her
for several minutes, then sighed. "I could hold you like this
orever, but I think we'd better get out of here before the
torm gets any worse."

Ginger stepped away from him and picked up Mischief,
then looked around. "I hope you know the way. I haven't a
clue to where we are."

"We'll just go back along the deer trail." Justin grinned
as he tucked Jo-Jo under his jacket, then put an arm around
Ginger. "We'll make it all right."

"I know we will." Ginger looked up at him, suddenly re-
lizing exactly how much he meant to her. "Together, we
can do anything, Justin."

"Even find a way to build a life together?" Justin took a
deep breath. This wasn't exactly the romantic setting he'd
had in mind as he drove out to the inn, but it was time to
admit his mistakes and find a way to make this woman his
orever. "I called your friend Toby yesterday, Ginger. Dena

told me about him and he says that factory is still available
I figure I can move production of my regular line out ther
and keep the fun new design production here where I hav
my best work force.''

"But I thought you didn't want to expand." Ginge
slowed, hope pounding through her, instantly banishing he
awareness of the increasing rain. "You said—"

"I said a lot of things, but that was before I realized wha
life would be like without you. I still think Willow Ru
should be our main home, but if I'm going to have a wif
who is a California management mogul, I better hav
something out there to keep me busy while she's mogu
ing." He stopped to look at her. "Am I going to have a wife
Ginger?"

"I love you, Justin, but . . ." The word *marriage* brough
all the old familiar doubts back to haunt her. Marryin
Justin sounded heavenly, but he was sure to want childrer
He would be a terrific father, but what if she was no bette
at mothering than her mother had been? What if . . .

"But what? If you love me, we can find a way, Ginger.
won't ask you to give up your company. I know how muc
it means to you. All I ask is that you share my life here, too
Is that too much?"

Ginger forced her doubts away, aware that to love mear
to trust. She had to trust Justin's love and her own. "I war
a life with you. I want to be a part of Willow Run and th
inn and everything here, but I'm not sure I can fit in. I ju
don't want to cheat you out of the happiness you deserve.

"The only way you can do that is if you won't try, Gi
ger. Loving you and building a family with you is the mo
important thing in the world to me. I promise to do my be
to make you happy, but unless you want that, too, it won
work. Do you want to share a life with me? Can you be
lieve that our love is strong enough to make it work?''

She met his gaze, her heart swelling with the tide of love that swept through her. "I want to spend the rest of my life loving you. And I know that as long as we're together, we can do anything."

"Then let's get Jo-Jo home and head for the inn where we can build a fire and settle down to make some wedding plans."

"And maybe a few calls?" Ginger snuggled against his side as they hurried through the gathering darkness. "Aunt Dena and Mom are going to be thrilled to hear our plans. I think they knew we were in love even before we did."

"Before either of us was willing to admit it, anyway," Justin agreed. "I think I've always loved you— I was just afraid to admit it, even to myself."

"And I was afraid to love anyone. I never believed I had enough love to give." Her heart grew lighter with that admission.

"I think we can prove how wrong you were about that later." Justin stopped long enough to give her a light kiss of promise. "But first, we've got to get in out of the cold."

"Right." Ginger agreed easily, but inside she knew that the warmth of Justin's love was all the protection she would ever need.

Epilogue

The late-afternoon sunlight bathed the stone-and-log inn with a Maytime glow as Justin parked in the empty parking lot. "So what do you think, Mrs. McGovern—isn't this a better place to start our honeymoon than a hotel in Denver?"

"Are you serious, Justin? A couple of weeks ago when I asked Dena about spending our wedding night here, she said that the inn wasn't quite ready for guests." Ginger brushed more of the birdseed their friends had showered them with from her green going-away suit as she turned to meet her new husband's gaze.

Justin chuckled, then touched his lips to hers. "I asked her to tell everyone that, so we could have the place all to ourselves, no interruptions. I mean, what do we need people for? Your Mom and Dena promised to stock the refrigerator with food and champagne. What else could we want?"

"I don't want or need anything but you, Justin." Ginger's eyes blurred with tears of joy as Justin helped her from the car, then kept his arm around her as they climbed the stairs to the inn door.

Ginger rested her cheek against his shoulder, enjoying the misty feeling of complete happiness. On her wedding day she had a right to be a little overemotional. She hadn't even minded that Justin teased her about crying when Dena told her that Mischief would have a special wedding gift for them—the pick of the litter Mischief and Jo-Jo were expecting any day now.

"At least I can promise that we won't have to make do with blankets in front of the fire tonight, my love. While you were off in California taking care of our businesses, I made a few special arrangements of my own." Justin opened the door, then picked her up in his arms. "Since this is where we first found love, it seems like the perfect place to begin our married life."

"Romantic and right. Oh, Justin, how did you know that I've always dreamed..." Ginger buried her fingers in his midnight hair, then found his lips for a kiss that left her dizzy with desire.

"We share the same dreams, love, haven't you realized that yet? And now we're about to make the best one come true." Justin's voice was rough with passion as he tightened his embrace and carried her across the vast lobby and up the stairway.

Ginger held her breath as memories of her long-ago dream filled her mind. Would he choose that room?

He did, and she gasped in delight as she saw the gleaming brass bed, the covers turned back and a rose on the pillow. "Oh, Justin, it's a dream come true, my dream...."

"This is no dream, Ginger." He set her gently on her feet, then began to unbutton her jacket, his hands trembling slightly with his own pent-up passion. "My love is real and forever." His lips found hers in a kiss that delved the depths of her flaring desire.

"I'm not sure forever will be long enough." Ginger unbuttoned his shirt and pressed her damp lips to his throat, feeling the surge of his racing pulse as it matched hers. His hands moved over her slowly, undressing her with tenderness. His lips followed, caressing her until she could no longer bear the madness of wanting him.

"Love me, Justin," she whispered, pulling him down onto the bed with her. "Love me now and forever, as I'll love you."

"As we'll love each other." His lips claimed hers once again as her dream finally came true.

*   *   *   *   *

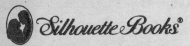

Take 4 bestselling love stories FREE

Plus get a FREE surprise gift!

Special Limited-time Offer

Silhouette Reader Service®

Mail to

In the U.S.
3010 Walden Avenue
P.O. Box 1867
Buffalo, N.Y. 14269-1867

In Canada
P.O. Box 609
Fort Erie, Ontario
L2A 5X3

YES! Please send me 4 free Silhouette Romance® novels and my free surprise gift. Then send me 6 brand-new novels every month, which I will receive months before they appear in bookstores. Bill me at the low price of $2.25* each. There are no shipping, handling or other hidden costs. I understand that accepting the books and gift places me under no obligation ever to buy any books. I can always return a shipment and cancel at any time. Even if I never buy another book from Silhouette, the 4 free books and the surprise gift are mine to keep forever.

*Offer slightly different in Canada—$2.25 per book plus 69¢ per shipment for delivery.
Sales tax applicable in N.Y. Canadian residents add applicable federal and provincial sales tax.

215 BPA HAYY (US)   315 BPA 8176 (CAN)

Name	(PLEASE PRINT)

Address	Apt. No.

City	State/Prov.	Zip/Postal Code

This offer is limited to one order per household and not valid to present Silhouette Romance® subscribers. Terms and prices are subject to change.

SROM-BPADR   © 1990 Harlequin Enterprises Limited

K

IT'S A CELEBRATION OF MOTHERHOOD!

Following the success of BIRDS, BEES and BABIES, we are proud to announce our second collection of Mother's Day stories.

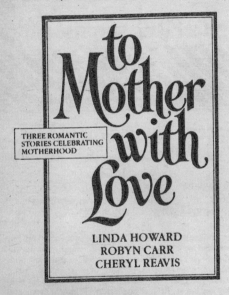

THREE ROMANTIC STORIES CELEBRATING MOTHERHOOD

to Mother with Love

LINDA HOWARD
ROBYN CARR
CHERYL REAVIS

Three stories in one volume, all by award-winning authors—stories especially selected to reflect the love all families share.

Available in May, TO MOTHER WITH LOVE is a perfect gift for yourself or a loved one to celebrate the joy of motherhood.

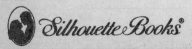

Silhouette Books®

ML-1